He'd been crazy about this woman.

She'd been everything Cade had ever dreamed of. Sexy as hell, with a passion that left him reeling. And he'd been so sure he'd found the one woman who understood him, the one who really cared.

He'd been wrong.

But now, lying beside her and listening to her soft breathing, it was hard to forget the good parts of their marriage. The easy camaraderie. The trust.

He gazed up at the stars and wondered for the hundredth time what had gone wrong—why she'd left him. He knew she'd hated being alone, but he'd never expected her to leave. He closed his eyes and listened to her drift into sleep. So why had she gone?

Even after all this time, he still didn't know the answer.

Dear Reader,

Leaping from an airplane into the slipstream, hurtling ninety miles an hour toward the fiery earth—who are these amazing people who risk their lives to fight fires? Smoke jumpers, of course—the elite men and women of the wildfire-fighting world.

What a privilege it was for me to meet these courageous people while I was researching this book. They impressed me with their commitment to catching fire, their camaraderie, their willingness to work under the most harrowing conditions while putting their lives on the line. And I now have a much deeper appreciation for the risks they take to save our lands.

I hope you enjoy this glimpse into the smoke jumpers' dangerous world and join me in thanking them for all they do. They are truly American heroes.

Happy reading!

Gail Barrett

Facing the FIRE

GAIL BARRETT

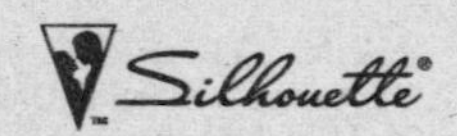

INTIMATE MOMENTS™

Published by Silhouette Books

America's Publisher of Contemporary Romance

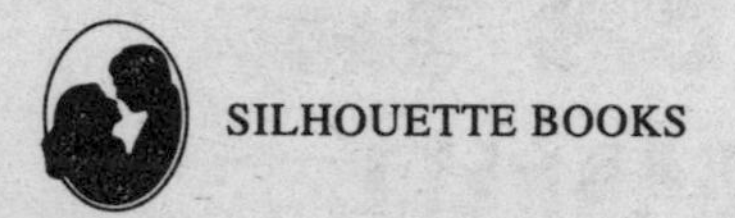

ISBN 0-373-27484-X

FACING THE FIRE

This edition published by arrangement with Harlequin Books S.A.

Visit Silhouette Books at www.eHarlequin.com

Printed in U.S.A.

Books by Gail Barrett

Silhouette Intimate Moments

Facing the Fire #1414

Silhouette Special Edition

Where He Belongs #1722

GAIL BARRETT

always dreamed of becoming a writer. After living everywhere from Spain to the Bahamas, raising two children and teaching high school Spanish for years, she finally fulfilled that lifelong goal. Her writing has won numerous awards, including Romance Writers of America's prestigious Golden Heart. Gail currently lives in western Maryland with her two sons, a quirky Chinook dog and her own Montana rancher-turned-retired Coast Guard officer hero. Write to her at P.O. Box 65, Funkstown, Maryland 21734-0065, or visit her Web site, www.gailbarrett.com.

To my mother for all those trips to the library, where I discovered the magical world of books, and to my dad for attending everything, even the bagpipe competitions. Your support matters more than you know.

ACKNOWLEDGMENTS:

Special thanks again to Forest Service spokesman Tim Eldridge for answering my endless questions, and to smoke jumpers everywhere for everything you do. You are amazing!

Chapter 1

Jordan Wells lifted the old metal bucket out of the icy stream and set it beside her on the bank. Shivering, she rubbed her wet, chilled hands on her jeans to warm them. She'd forgotten how cold these Montana streams were. They were little more than glacial melt rushing down the mountains.

But the place was beautiful, she had to admit. Smiling, she glanced around the tiny clearing. Early-afternoon sunlight sifted through the Douglas fir trees, making the water sparkle. The clear stream raced over rocks and overturned pebbles while the pine boughs moaned above.

She inhaled the deep-forest air, that complex mix of ancient pines and earth, so unlike the cornfields and woods of Virginia. She'd loved this place once. Being here had filled her with peace, serenity. She'd felt protected from the world, sheltered in the tiny cabin with Cade.

She closed her eyes and, just for a moment, let the images swamp her. Cade's hard face. His low, rough voice. That devastating grin.

The shocking thrills, the wild excitement she'd felt in his strong arms.

But that was before the fire season had started and the loneliness set in. The weeks apart. The endless waiting. Never knowing when he'd come back or how long he would stay.

Then the pleading. The desperation. That stark white hospital bed.

The shattering realization that he loved leaping out of airplanes more than he loved her. And always would.

She opened her eyes with a sigh. But that had happened years ago. That life was gone forever, like the innocent, trusting girl she'd once been.

And that was exactly why she'd come back here. To put that painful past to rest forever and prove she was over Cade. To sell the cabin she'd ignored for years and finally move on with her life. To marry Phil, a stable, steady man with a normal job who'd never rush off on wild adventures and leave her to suffer alone. Who'd waited far too patiently for too many months for her to accept his proposal.

And she would finally say yes to him. She'd be crazy not to. That man was everything she wanted.

She'd accept, all right. As soon as she cleaned out the cabin, she'd stop at the real estate agency in Missoula, sign the contract to sell this place and catch the next flight back East.

She rose and lifted the dented bucket. The thick bed of pine needles muffled her footsteps as she trudged up the narrow trail toward the house.

The wind gusted in the pine trees again and they creaked and wailed overhead. The tinge of wood smoke wafted past and Jordan paused. Had someone built a cabin nearby? She hadn't noticed any new side roads or even tire tracks on the long drive in. Maybe a passing hiker had started a campfire despite the burning ban.

Then she caught the distant buzz of an airplane and her breath stalled. A DC3 jump ship. She'd recognize that sound anywhere. She'd heard that sad, wrenching drone every time Cade flew away.

Her heart pumping hard against her ribs, she set the bucket on the ground and looked up. A patch of blazing blue sky peeked through the thrashing pines.

Could there be a fire nearby? Fear crawled down her spine. How would she know? Her cell phone didn't work out here so she couldn't call to find out, and no one knew where she was. She listened intently, but the lonely sound drifted away.

She inhaled deeply, but only smelled fresh air and pine. She eased her breath back out. It was just her imagination. Old ghosts. The very memories she'd come here to banish.

She picked up the bucket and carted it into the cabin. Old ghosts or not, she'd better finish quickly and leave.

Cade McKenzie stood in the open doorway of the DC3 and sucked in the smell of burning pine. Below him, black, roiling smoke pierced by huge orange flames rose from the Montana forest and covered the earth with a threatening shadow.

Undaunted, he snapped down his face guard and narrowed his eyes. No matter how formidable the fire, he'd stop it. The steep hills and volatile winds only challenged him more. And he knew the eleven smokejumpers poised behind him felt the same.

The spotter, hanging partway out the door beside him, pulled in his head from the slipstream. "Hold into the wind," he shouted over the roar of the rushing air. "And stay wide of the fire. It's gusting bad down low."

Cade nodded and returned his attention to the fire. They would jump near the heel and contain it first, then split up and secure the flanks. Despite the dry conditions, they could pinch off the head by late tomorrow—unless the wind changed direction and whipped the flames toward Granite Canyon.

His gaze shifted west toward the canyon bordered by a silver ridge. From the air, the dense pines hid the log cabin he knew was nestled beside the boulders. His old cabin, where he'd spent the most intoxicating months of his life—until Jordan decided she couldn't handle living with a smokejumper and cleared out. A sharp stab of bitterness tightened his gut. Hell of a time to think of his ex-wife.

He forced the old anger aside. She'd raked him over good, all right, but he'd never see her again. She wouldn't have kept the cabin after all these years. Still, he needed to make sure no one was in there in case the wind switched and the fire jumped the only road out.

"We're on final." The spotter scooted back and struck

the side of the open door. His adrenaline rising, Cade moved forward into jump position. His jump partner, a rookie from a booster crew out of Boise, pressed in close behind him.

His muscles bunched, his gaze focused on the horizon, he waited for the spotter's signal. An intense calm settled over him and his mind stilled.

And in that moment, he felt perfectly right. He was doing what he was born for, what he loved.

The spotter slapped his calf hard. His pulse jerked. He thrust himself out of the plane and into the roaring slipstream. And hurtled ninety miles an hour toward the fiery earth.

The wind rose again, swirling the orange flames high and pushing sparks and smoke over the line. Cade cut off his chain saw and lifted his arm to wipe the sweat dripping down his cheeks beneath his hard hat.

Something wasn't right; he could feel it. But what? They'd secured the heel without problems and begun scratching a line up both flanks. But instead of feeling confident they would slay this dragon, unease slid through his gut. And he'd fought fires for too many years to ignore his instincts.

Unsettled, he strode to the pile of equipment and set down his saw, then pulled his canteen from his personal-gear bag. He drank deeply, letting the warm water soothe his parched throat.

"Hey, Cade."

His smokejumping bro, Trey Campbell, strolled over. They'd rookied the same year out of Missoula and jumped together ever since. And after Jordan had deserted him, they'd spent more nights than he could remember frequenting Montana's bars.

Trey rummaged in his own bag and pulled out his water. "Any word on this wind?" he asked.

"No, but it feels like it's picking up." He frowned back at the fire. Heavy brush and snags littered the forest floor, fueling the surging flames. The erratic wind kicked up sparks and slopped spot fires over the line.

He recapped his canteen, pulled out his radio and keyed the mike. "Dispatch, this is McKenzie."

His radio crackled. "Go ahead, McKenzie."

"Any idea what's going on with this wind? It's blowing the hell out of our line."

Voices murmured in the background. "We'll call the district for an update," the dispatcher said. "We'll get right back to you on that."

"Thanks." He stuffed the radio in the side pocket of his bag. "Do you mind taking over for awhile?" he asked Trey. "There's a cabin by the rim of the canyon I need to check out, make sure there aren't any people hanging around." Like his ex-wife? His stomach tightened but he quickly discounted that thought. "They're going to need a head start getting out of here if that wind shifts."

"That your old cabin by any chance?"

"Yeah." Which he'd surrendered to Jordan, along with any illusions he'd ever had about marriage. "After I swing by the cabin, I'll recon the head again, too. When dispatch gets back with that wind report, we can decide where to build line tonight."

"Got it." Trey's teeth flashed white in his soot-streaked face. He shoved his canteen into his personal-gear bag, picked up his chain saw, and loped back toward the line.

Cade took a final swallow of water, then stuffed his canteen in his own personal-gear bag. He moved a small notebook and compass to the side pocket with the radio, and secured the flap.

A sudden blur in his peripheral vision caught his attention and he glanced up. A blazing snag pitched silently forward, and his heart stopped.

A widow maker. A dead, burning tree that fell without warning, killing anyone in its path. And it was heading straight for their line.

"Watch out," he shouted. "A snag!"

The men immediately scattered—except for one. His jump partner, the rookie. The kid looked up, then froze.

Oh, hell. Cade lunged to his feet and sprinted forward. The tree toppled closer and his adrenaline surged. With a final burst of speed, he barreled into the rookie and knocked him out of the way.

And was instantly slammed to the ground.

His breath fled as a massive weight crushed his back. He struggled to lift his face from the dirt, but branches covered his head.

He couldn't see. He couldn't breathe. Where was the rookie? He tried to shout, but couldn't move his mouth.

He shoved against the ground but the branches trapped him. Heat blazed up his back and his adrenaline rose. He pushed again, his efforts futile against the punishing weight.

"Cade! Are you okay? Oh, God. Get him out!"

"We need saws in here," someone else yelled over the roar. "Hurry up!"

Cade's eyes burned. He choked down hot smoke and coughed. Heat crawled up his neck and he gasped for breath.

Chain saws wailed and men shouted. The weight shifted slightly and the branches thrashed above him. Then suddenly, they were gone.

He lifted his head and sucked in air. Work boots stood inches from his face, along with green Nomex pants.

"Oh, man," the rookie said, his voice trembling. "Are you okay?"

"Don't touch him." Trey crouched beside him. "Speak to me, buddy."

"I'm fine," Cade managed.

"Are you sure?" the rookie asked. "Man, that was close."

"Damn close," Trey said. "He's lucky the trunk missed him. If he'd been one second slower…"

But he'd escaped, and so had the rookie. "Thanks, guys." He struggled to push himself upright. Pain knifed his shoulder and he hitched in a ragged breath.

"Hold on. We'll help you up," Trey said.

"I can do it." He wasn't injured, for God's sake. He just needed to catch his breath. "Just get a line around that snag before it spreads the fire."

He forced himself to his knees. Nausea roiled through his belly, but he ignored it and stood.

He waited until the ground steadied and the chain saws started up again. Then, his head down, his right shoulder throbbing, he staggered off the line. His pulse lurched. His skull hammered. Sweat and ash stung his eyes.

The rookie stayed with him. "I still can't believe how fast that fell. I didn't even hear it coming."

Cade stopped near the pile of equipment. He inhaled, and pain seared straight to his ribs.

"Man, do I owe you," the rookie continued. "I can't believe I froze like that."

"Forget it."

"No, really. If you hadn't pushed me out of the way—"

"We'd be peeling your skin off that stob," Trey said from behind them. "Look, we'll do the play-by-play later. Grab a Pulaski and help get that damned thing inside the line."

"Sure." The rookie grabbed the ax-like Pulaski. "Thanks again, man. I owe you." He turned and trotted off.

Cade tipped back his head. Even that small movement made him grimace.

"We'd better look at that shoulder," Trey said.

"I'm fine. I just need to catch my breath." He bent to grab his canteen, then froze as his back and ribs pulsed.

Angry now, he straightened. A wave of dizziness blurred his eyes.

"Come on, Cade. You know the rules."

He knew the drill, all right. Safety first. Get an injured man off the mountain. Anyone who couldn't outrun a fire endangered himself and the other jumpers.

And he was far too professional to compromise his men.

But he wasn't seriously injured. His shoulder was

probably just wrenched. And smokejumpers worked hurt all the time. Bad knees, sprained ankles… Chronic pain came with the job.

Besides, he couldn't leave the fire—his fire. Not until they had it under control.

And those damn doctors. What if they took him off the jump list? Hell! He couldn't stop jumping now, not with fires raging all over the west.

Not ever. Dread rolled through his gut. "Just give me a minute," he said. "I'll shake it off." He reached up to remove his hard hat. Pain flamed through his shoulder and he dropped his hand. He glanced at Trey and saw the doubt in his eyes.

"We can't wait," Trey said. "If this wind picks up, they'll ground the choppers. We need to call it in now."

"A few more minutes won't matter. Look, I'll go check out that cabin and make sure no one's hanging around. If my shoulder isn't better by then, I'll call it in myself."

"Cade—"

"For God's sake. Nothing's broken." With supreme effort, he picked up his PG bag and swung it over his left shoulder. Sweat popped out on his forehead and he struggled to breathe.

Trey shook his head. "All right, but I'm going with you, and we'll scout a landing spot on the way."

"Fine." He hated pulling a man off the line, but didn't bother to argue. He knew he'd need every bit of breath he had for the steep trek to the cabin.

By the time they reached Granite Canyon, Cade could hardly stay upright. His head reeled, hot pain ripped through his shoulder, and his ribs burned whenever he breathed.

He stopped at the black Jeep Liberty parked under the trees and propped himself against it to catch his breath.

"You okay?" Trey asked.

"A little winded." He blinked to clear his blurred vision.

"McKenzie?" a voice on his radio called.

"I'll see who's in the cabin," Trey said.

"Go ahead." Glad to have an excuse to lean against the Jeep, Cade pulled his radio from his bag. "McKenzie here."

"This is dispatch. We got that weather report you wanted."

"Good. What's the forecast?" He watched Trey stride to the door.

"Right now it's holding steady at fifteen knots, with gusts up to twenty-five. But there's a front coming through…."

The cabin door opened. A tall, slender woman stepped out and her dark hair gleamed in the light. Trey shifted sideways, and Cade caught sight of her face.

His heart stalled. His chest cramped tight, and suddenly, he felt dazed, as if the tree had crushed him again.

His gaze swept over her features. Those dark, exotic eyes. That full, erotic mouth. And damned if he didn't still feel that pull, that powerful lure of passion and innocence that had once demolished his heart.

He scowled. Innocence, hell. She was as helpless as a rattler, and about as trustworthy, too.

She looked past Trey and their gazes latched. Her dark eyes widened and she mouthed his name.

Bitterness seeped through his gut. His ex-wife. Just what he'd needed to cap off a hell of a day.

"Did you get that?" the person on the radio asked.

"Yeah, I heard you." He turned his back on his ex-wife. The motion set off another wave of dizziness. "Listen. There's a Forest Service road that runs just north of the fire, then intersects with Highway 10. Is it still clear?"

"It is for now. In an hour it could get dicey. The front's going to push that way."

Unless they stopped the fire first.

"Okay. Let me know if anything changes. We've got a civilian heading out that way." He turned the radio to scan.

Trey jogged over. "She's packing up now. She'll be out of here in just a few minutes."

"Great." He shoved his radio into his bag and sharp pain jolted his shoulder. He sucked in his breath.

"Some shock seeing her again," Trey added.

"Yeah." Shock didn't begin to describe it. He felt that familiar anger blaze through him, the same rage and resentment that had consumed him for months. The fury that he'd let himself be conned by a pretty face in search of an easy paycheck. And had convinced himself it was love.

"How's the shoulder?" Trey asked.

He brought his attention back to his job. Smokejumping. Fighting fire. The only thing that mattered. Everything he was.

But he had to face the harsh truth. He couldn't work this fire with his body in this condition, and refusing to leave could endanger the troops.

"It hurts like hell," he admitted. "My collarbone's probably cracked. I'd better get it checked."

"Do you want me to call for a chopper?"

"There's no place to land. The nearest clearing's a mile up that ridge." He'd hiked this forest enough to know.

"So we cut a spot."

"We don't have time. A front's moving in. If we don't get that fire stopped now it could go big." Which would endanger the men even more. And he could never live with himself if that happened.

"So what do you suggest?" Trey asked.

What else could he do? The men couldn't afford to waste valuable time clearing a landing pad, and he couldn't get himself to that ridge.

He glanced at the Jeep. Dread churned through his gut and the bitter taste of gall filled his mouth.

It had been one hell of a day, all right. And it was about to get even worse.

He slowly turned back to the cabin. The door opened and Jordan stepped out, carrying a bag. He smiled grimly. "It looks like I'm going to hitch myself a ride."

Chapter 2

Still reeling from the shock of seeing Cade again, Jordan loaded the last of her belongings in the back of the Jeep and shut the hatch. She'd never expected to see him here. Never. And now she was going to spend six hours with him in the Jeep? Good God. Dealing with his memory had been hard enough.

She lifted her stunned gaze to her ex-husband. He stood at the front of the Jeep with Trey, examining a map spread over the hood. While she'd packed up the few blankets and bowls worth saving from the cabin, they'd pored over the map, discussing wind speed and fire retardant.

Cade's hard hat dipped as he folded the map and tucked it into his PG bag. Then he pulled out a battery pack and handed it to Trey. "You might as well take my spares," he said. "You could be out here for a while."

His deep, sensual voice drew goose bumps along her arms, and despite the warm wind, she shivered. God, she'd once loved that voice. It was the first thing she'd noticed about him in that smoky Mexican bar.

The first of many. He stepped away from the Jeep and her gaze drifted over the rest of him. Ashes dusted his battered boots. His olive drab pants rode low on his lean hips and his yellow fire shirt stretched wide across his shoulders. He looked broader through the chest than before, his neck thicker.

Her pulse fluttered. Even in his early twenties, he'd been a gorgeous man. But now…

Now he was simply a smokejumper who needed a ride.

Trey nodded in her direction. "Thanks for helping us out here."

"Sure. No problem." Trey headed toward the trees, and her pulse faltered. No problem? When she was alone in the forest with Cade?

She slid her gaze to her ex-husband, and those shocking blue eyes met hers. Her heart lurched, then wobbled madly. Oh, God, those eyes. How could she have forgotten? That brilliant blue. That carnal gleam. And when he'd smiled… She'd taken one fatal look in that Cancún bar and fallen hard.

But he didn't smile at her now. His gaze slammed into hers, narrow and cold, as stark as the grim lines bracketing his mouth. Harsh, like the chiseled cheekbones streaked with dirt and the hard jaw lined with blond stubble.

He strode toward her and her nerves climbed higher. She scanned his face, searching for a hint of warmth.

His mouth flattened, and her hopes tumbled. So much for a friendly ride.

He stopped at the rear passenger door, his stony gaze locked on hers. "You ready?"

"Yes."

"Good." He dropped his PG bag to the ground, yanked open the door with his left hand and hefted the bag to the seat. Still using the same hand, he pulled off his hard hat, dumped it beside the bag, and slammed the door. Then he opened the front passenger door and bent his long frame to climb in the Jeep. He froze with a rough gasp of breath.

And suddenly, it hit her. No wonder he wanted a ride. He was injured—and badly, if it had made him leave his job. The job he'd loved more than her.

She quickly moved behind him. "Can I help?"

"No."

"But your arm—"

"It's fine."

Uncertain, she stepped back. He pulled himself inside the Jeep and awkwardly reached for the door.

"Here, let me—" She started to close it, but his hard stare stopped her cold. "Fine." She lifted her hands and backed off, then stalked to the driver's-side door. Let him fend for himself if he was too proud to accept any help.

Too proud or too bitter?

She slid behind the wheel and braved a glance at the man slumped beside her. His skin looked ashen beneath the grime, his profile strained. The faint scent of wood smoke permeated his clothes.

She shook her head. Why would he be angry? He was the one who'd abandoned her. He'd flown off with that booster crew to Alaska, just when she'd needed him most.

She blocked off a swell of resentment. It didn't matter anymore. Their marriage was over, and had been since the day he'd left for refresher training.

Besides, she had her life in Virginia now—a good one, too, including a man who'd never leave her. All she had to do was drive Cade back to Missoula and then she'd never see him again.

She inhaled deeply, cranked the engine to life and slowly released the clutch. The Jeep lurched forward, hit a downed branch, and jostled sideways.

She glanced at Cade. The grooves deepened around his mouth and his skin paled even more. "Are you going to be okay?" she asked.

"Yeah."

Her nerves tightened. Maybe he was all right, but she had a feeling this was going to be the longest six hours of her life.

The Jeep had stopped moving. Disoriented, Cade forced open his eyes and blinked hard to clear his blurred vision. They were parked in the middle of the narrow dirt road, surrounded by towering pines. The driver's door hung open and the warm wind ruffled a paper napkin on the console. Jordan was nowhere in sight.

He lifted his hand to rub his eyes, then froze as pain sliced his shoulder. *Damn.* That tree had slammed him good. His skull vibrated like the two-stroke engine of a chain saw, and his entire body felt pummeled.

He glanced at his watch, then slumped back against the seat and shut his eyes. They'd only been driving for a few minutes. He'd either passed out or fallen asleep as soon as they'd left the cabin.

But where was Jordan? And why weren't they moving? He jerked his eyes open again. This was a hell of a time to take a break. They needed to get out of here before the wind picked up and pushed the fire to the road.

Stifling a groan, he reached over with his left hand and shoved his door open, then swung out his legs and stepped down. Dizziness swamped him, and he hung on to the door to catch his balance. Several breaths later, the ground steadied and he slowly straightened.

"Don't shut the door," Jordan said, her voice low.

Startled, he turned toward the back of the Jeep. Jordan knelt in the road facing the woods. His gaze followed the curve of her slender back to the lush flare of her hips. Her faded blue jeans were covered with dust.

"What are you doing?"

"Sshh." She rose to her feet and backed toward him. "I'm trying to catch a dog."

"What?"

"Quiet! You'll scare him off."

He frowned at the bowl of water she'd set on the road next to what looked like pieces of sandwich. He followed her line of vision to the trees but couldn't see anything.

He massaged his eyes. "How long ago did we stop?"

"I don't know. Maybe fifteen minutes."

"Fifteen minutes?" *Hell.* They were far too close to the cabin. "Listen—"

"Shh. Here he comes."

A clump of ferns edging the road swayed, and then a dog slunk out. At least he thought it was a dog. It was the scrawniest thing he'd ever seen, with wary, desperate eyes set in a gaunt face hollowed by hunger.

"I almost hit him," she murmured. "He was sitting right in the road."

The dog limped closer, favoring his right front paw, then stopped several yards away. Trembling, his tail tucked to his belly and dark ears flattened, he again inched cautiously forward. His eyes darted from them to the food and he let out a pitiful whine.

"I thought he was a coyote at first," she said, her voice low.

"Coyotes are fatter than that."

"That's why I decided he was a dog. Either he's lost or someone dumped him off in the forest. As if a pet can survive out here by instinct."

Her indignation didn't surprise him. She'd always had a soft spot for animals, even wild ones. When they'd lived at the cabin, she'd hung bird feeders in the woods and set salt licks out for the deer.

He turned his attention back to the dog, who was creeping toward the food. He was some sort of shepherd mix, with a matted, tawny coat and dark gray mask and ears. The dog reached the food and stopped. Then suddenly, he bolted back to the woods.

Cade glanced at his watch again. "Okay, let's go."

"Go?" Jordan frowned. "But what about the dog?"

"He'll eat as soon as we leave."

"And then what? Where's he going to get more food?" She planted her hands on her hips. The motion tightened the white T-shirt over her breasts. "You saw how skinny he is. And he needs to get to a vet. That front paw doesn't look good."

"We don't have a choice. We need to get out of here before that front hits."

"But we can't just leave him here alone."

That figured. She cared more about leaving a stray dog than she once had about her husband. "For God's sake—"

"Forget it, Cade. I'm not leaving that poor dog behind. He's already been abandoned once, and believe me, that's enough for anyone." Her dark eyes flashed. "Not that you'd understand that."

Not that he'd understand what? "What the hell does that mean?"

"Nothing."

"The hell it doesn't." His irritation surged.

She lifted her hands and sighed. "All right, fine. I'll tell you. It's just that you're always flying off and traveling somewhere. Having adventures and putting out fires. You don't know what it's like to be left behind, to be sitting at home waiting, day after lonely day. But I do. And believe me, I'm not doing that to the dog."

He stared at her in disbelief. "What are you talking about? You're the one who left me."

"Only because you'd already gone."

Incredulity flooded through him. He would have laughed if his ribs didn't ache so much. "Hell, that's rich. You walk out without even a note. I come home to an empty house and a goddamn letter from your lawyer. And you accuse me of abandoning you?"

"You went to Alaska."

He stared at her. "I was working. Earning money. You know, trying to support my wife?"

Her brows rose. "You're not seriously saying you were doing it for my sake?"

"Hell, yes, I was doing it for you. Wasn't I supposed to work?"

"But you were gone all the time. You hardly came back. You even joined that booster crew to Alaska."

"That was my job," he said tightly. "You knew that when we got married. The Forest Service owns you in the summer. They send you wherever the fires are. You can't control where you go. And you can't just turn work down."

"You could have found a different job."

"Right." That was their problem, right there. Ten years ago, he'd idolized this woman. Worshipped her. Given her his heart, his soul. Everything he owned and every damned cent he earned. And she still hadn't been satisfied. She'd wanted him to change who he was.

She bit her lip. Her dark eyes widened with that vulnerable look that always made him want to protect her.

His jaw flexed. She knew exactly how to play him, all right. Even knowing the truth, how she'd ripped out his heart and screwed him over, he had the ridiculous urge to console her.

Well, she'd suckered him in once with that helpless act. Damned if he would fall for it again.

She sighed. "Look. Can we just forget it? I don't want to argue all the way to Missoula."

"Yeah." He didn't need this aggravation. He had

enough problems to deal with. He needed to hightail it back to Missoula and get himself checked by a doctor so he could return to the jump list.

"Catching the dog won't take that long," she added. "I'm sure he was somebody's pet."

"We've already stayed here too long. That road's going to close any minute."

"Is the fire really that close?"

He glanced at the thrashing treetops. "It depends on the wind speed, but yeah, it's almost here."

"But what's the dog going to do in the fire?" Her dark eyes pleaded with his. "He can't run with that hurt paw. And he's so hungry."

"He'll get away." He returned his gaze to the dog skulking from the safety of the trees. Despite his assurances, they both knew that he wouldn't make it. He was far too weak to escape a wildfire.

"Just give me five more minutes." Her soft brown eyes met his again, and despite the urgency, he felt himself waver. "Please?"

He pulled his gaze from hers and back to the swaying pine trees. He was a damn fool, risking his life for a stray mutt and a woman who had betrayed him. But crazy or not, the sooner they captured that dog, the faster they could leave the forest.

"Three," he told her. "And not a second more." Resigned, he opened the rear passenger door and riffled through his PG bag. He found his supply of beef jerky in the side compartment, removed several strips and handed them to Jordan. "Here. If this doesn't get him, nothing will."

"Thanks." Her full mouth softened into a smile, and he felt the tug to his heart.

He was a fool, all right. Annoyed by his weakness for this woman, he strode to the front of the Jeep. Then he propped himself against it to wait.

Jordan walked to the edge of the road, broke off a piece of beef jerky and tossed it to the dog. The dog eyed it and scented the air. The warm wind blew dried pine needles across the road and lifted the fur on his ruff. After several seconds, he padded forward and licked the jerky, then finally gulped it down.

Jordan held out another piece. "Come on, sweetie," she cooed. "Come here. We won't hurt you."

Without warning, Cade felt the caress of her soft voice, remembered it sliding over him in the dark, along with her lips and body. His gaze roved her tiny waist, the curve of her bottom encased in tight blue jeans, the pale patch of skin exposed beneath the T-shirt. He wanted to run his hands up that silken skin, taste her heat, her desire. Hear that low moan she made when he stroked her naked breasts.

He dragged in his breath. This was a hell of a time to remember their sex life—the one thing they'd gotten exactly right.

He forced his attention back to the dog. Looking as mesmerized as Cade had once been by Jordan's voice, the dog crept cautiously closer. But he stopped a few feet from her hand.

Cade's admiration rose. The dog was smarter than he'd ever been. That sexy voice wouldn't trap him.

"Come here," Jordan wheedled. The dog whined,

and she tossed him another piece of jerky. Still trembling, he again inched forward. Then he snatched up the jerky and ate it.

"That's right," Jordan encouraged. She held out another piece. "You're such a sweetie. Such a good dog."

The dog moved even closer. Just inches from her hand, he stopped, plopped his hindquarters in the dust and craned his neck toward her hand.

"Look, he has a collar. He really was someone's pet."

"Jordan—"

"I know. We're almost there. Such a good dog," she continued cooing. Seconds later, the dog scooted forward and took the beef from her hand. "Good boy! Now let's get you in the car. Come on, sweetie. Come on." Holding another fragment of jerky, she backed slowly to the Jeep. The dog glanced at Cade and yawned.

"Look away," she said.

"What?"

"You're stressing him out. Don't look him in the eyes. And yawn if you can. That will make him feel safer."

Skeptical, but willing to do anything to hurry them out of the forest, Cade turned his head and faked a yawn. In his peripheral vision, he saw the dog creep toward the Jeep, and his respect for Jordan grew. So she could manage dogs.

"Okay, this is the test." She set the jerky on the floor of the Jeep and stepped back. "Come on," she urged.

The wind creaked the pine branches in the silence. The dog limped forward, then stopped. Seconds ticked by, and Cade's impatience mounted. But just as he opened his mouth to protest, the dog jumped into the Jeep.

Jordan closed the door. "Got him." She whirled around and beamed up at him, and he felt the kick to his heart. "That beef jerky was perfect. What a great idea."

"I guess he just needed the right enticement." His gaze slid over her creamy face to the pale smattering of freckles on her nose, over soft, full lips and down to her breasts. His pulse leaped. He knew what had motivated him.

Until she'd gutted his heart and stomped out his illusions. His jaw hardened. "Let's get out of here."

"Sure." Hurt flashed in her eyes and she turned away.

Hell. He hadn't meant to sound rude, but he didn't have time to mince around her feelings. They had to get out of this forest fast.

While she retrieved the bowl she'd set in the road, he climbed into the Jeep and closed his door. The movement sent pain shooting through his shoulder and he struggled to breathe. As bad as he ached, he must have cracked his collarbone, maybe even a couple of ribs. Jordan slid in beside him and slammed her door, and the sound throbbed through his skull. He probably had a concussion, too. He just hoped it wouldn't keep him off the jump list long.

She cranked the engine and they lurched forward. Unable to buckle his seat belt, he planted his feet wide against the floorboard to steady himself in the seat. Fighting off another bout of dizziness, he closed his eyes.

For several moments, they drove in silence. Warm air rushed through the open windows. The Jeep bounced down the dusty road, eating up the distance toward the front. Like any seasoned smokejumper, Cade used the spare time to rest.

"Do you smell something?" Jordan asked.

He blinked open his eyes and sniffed. "Yeah. That damn dog stinks."

She shot him a wry smile. "I mean besides the dog. I could smell him out in the open." Her smile faded, and worry crept into her eyes. "I think I smell smoke."

He inhaled deeply this time, ignoring the ache in his ribs. The faint scent of burning pine filled his lungs. "Yeah, I smell it."

"Do you think we're too late to get through?"

"We'll find out." He scanned the thick trees lining the road but didn't see signs of the fire.

"I'll go faster." She accelerated, and the Jeep leaped forward. Dirt spun under the tires and kicked up clouds of dust. They hit a hard bump, jarring his shoulder, and he choked back a groan. He didn't care how much the damned thing throbbed. He'd have to wait and deal with it later, after they got past the fire.

The Jeep rocketed down the road and the smell of smoke grew stronger. Jordan stared straight ahead, her brow furrowed in concentration. Cade felt his own tension mount.

Then smoke drifted over the road and his stomach tightened. The fire was closer than he'd thought. And unless the front made a sharp detour, they'd be caught in its path.

They careened around a curve and up a knoll, and suddenly, the front appeared on the right. Deep-orange flames surged toward them. Dark, heavy smoke roiled over the road.

"Stop!"

Jordan slammed on the brakes. The Jeep skidded sideways, and Cade braced his boot against the dashboard to keep from hitting the windshield. They abruptly jerked to a stop.

The roar of the wildfire filled the forest. The wind whipped the tall flames skyward and curled them high through the trees. Dry branches exploded in brilliant bursts, shooting flames through the crowns.

"Oh, God," Jordan breathed.

Cade frowned. From what he could see through the smoke, the perimeter was completely erratic. Long fingers of flame ran ahead of the front, pushed by the powerful winds. Sparks blew through the billowing smoke and torched spot fires over the road.

A gust of wind scattered ashes on the Jeep. Flare-ups hissed and snapped beside them.

"Cade," Jordan said, her voice unsteady. "What are we going to do?"

Good question. "We can't outrun that flame front." Unless there was a natural barrier ahead that protected the road. And he sure as hell didn't remember one.

His shoulder screamed as he reached back for the radio in his PG bag and he blinked against the pain. Maybe someone had reconned the fire from the air and knew if they could make it. The smoke was too thick for him to tell from the ground.

But then the wind gusted again. The smoke lifted, and he saw the road for himself. It ran straight ahead, right into the path of the fire.

He glanced at Jordan. Raw fear shone in her eyes. "Can we get out?" she asked, her voice trembling.

His gut twisted, and he reluctantly shook his head. "Not through that. We're trapped."

Chapter 3

Trapped? Jordan tore her gaze from Cade and gaped at the inferno raging before her. A fierce roar shook the air. Flames swirled up pines like fiery tornadoes and shot sparks far overhead.

Fear slammed through her nerves and she stifled a cry. They had to get away. Run! But she couldn't move, couldn't breathe. Couldn't even see where they needed to go.

Ashes blew across the windshield and the grass beside the Jeep started burning. A towering wall of fire charged toward them while thick, heavy smoke rolled over the road.

"Turn around," Cade said over the noise.

"But the grass is burning!"

"So back up and then turn around."

Of course. Her heart hammering, her breathing shallow, she threw the Jeep into Reverse and hit the gas. They sped back to a wide spot in the road and she slammed on the brakes. The Jeep bucked to a stop, then stalled. "Oh, God."

"Take it easy," Cade said, his voice even. "We've got time."

Time? With the world around them on fire? She flicked her gaze to Cade. He slumped back in his seat, his head cradled casually against the headrest. How on earth could he stay so calm?

Her gaze switched to the windshield. The wild flames thundered over the earth, and terror raced through her chest. But Cade was right. This wasn't the time to panic. She needed to control her fear and get them away from this fire.

Inhaling deeply, she cranked the engine and spun the wheel, making the Jeep lurch forward. Then she hit the brakes, shoved the gearshift into Reverse and shot back.

They stopped, and she sucked in another breath. She'd turned the Jeep around. Now she just had to drive away. Her heart still sprinting, she floored the gas pedal. The Jeep fishtailed, straightened and hurtled back up the dirt road.

They rounded a bend, and she looked in the rearview mirror. The flames disappeared behind the dense stands of fir trees, and she hitched out her breath. They were safe, at least for now. She eased up her foot on the gas.

Several breaths later, her heart stopped quaking. She pried her fingers from the steering wheel and rearranged her grip. The roar of the fire gradually faded, and her galloping pulse finally slowed.

But then she heard a soft, high whistle from the backseat. She pulled her foot off the gas and glanced back.

The dog huddled on the floor behind Cade's seat, trembling wildly and breathing in thin, reedy gasps. "For goodness' sake," she said. He was hyperventilating. She reached back and stroked his soft head, and his worried gaze lifted to hers. "Don't worry, sweetie. We're okay."

At least she hoped so. She glanced at Cade, still slouched calmly in his seat, his booted feet planted on the floorboards. "What are we going to do now?"

His vibrant blue eyes met hers. "You remember that old logging trail past the cabin?"

"How could I forget it?" They'd hiked that trail dozens of times to picnic in the meadow by the stream.

At least they'd intended to picnic. Heat gathered low in her belly, along with a memory as intense as any fire. Of lying in the warm, sunlit grass, Cade's strong arms holding her tight. His hard face taut, his breathing ragged. His eyes singeing hers.

His blue eyes narrowed, and she knew he remembered it, too. Her heart thumped hard against her ribs and she yanked her gaze to the road.

"It might not be open," he continued, his voice rough. The husky timbre made her shiver. "I couldn't tell when we were setting up to jump. The timber's too heavy to see the road from the air."

"I guess we can give it a try."

"We don't have a choice. There aren't any other roads out here."

She tried to picture the abandoned road. She remembered long, deep ruts and knee-high weeds, at least in the section they'd hiked. They'd never quite made it past that meadow.

She cleared her throat. "Do you know where it comes out?"

"According to the map, it should hook on with another Forest Service road on the other side of the mountain. That's if we can get through."

"And if we can't?"

"We'll figure something out."

That remark was so typical of Cade that, despite her fear, the corner of her mouth curved up. "How many times have I heard that line?"

He lifted his uninjured shoulder, and she marveled again at his calm. He never worried or panicked, even with a forest fire licking his heels. He excelled when things got tough.

His confidence impressed her, though, and always had. And his strength. Her gaze slid down his corded neck and broad shoulders to those big, callused hands and muscled thighs. He was a tough, capable man, all right, and it had been easy to let him take charge.

But after he'd left, none of that strength had helped her. Not during the endless nights she'd spent alone. Not when she'd discovered she was pregnant. And especially not on the desperate drive to the hospital or in that cold, white hospital bed.

Or during the grief-stricken days that followed, when loss turned to desolation.

A hollow feeling filled her chest. She'd never told Cade about the baby. When he hadn't returned, she'd simply packed a bag and left, the same as he'd done to her.

A sliver of guilt pierced her throat. She knew she'd handled that badly. Instead of fleeing Missoula, she should have stayed and told him the truth. But she'd been nineteen years old, in an agony of pain, and so shattered she couldn't think straight.

And what did it matter now? The past was gone. And at least she'd learned her lesson. After suffering through a childhood with a wandering father and then that lonely marriage to Cade, she wanted a man who stayed home. And she'd have one, as soon as she got them out of the forest.

Her mind safely back on track, she drove quickly along the dusty road, past the spot where they'd rescued the dog. Minutes later, their old cabin came into view. Despite her neglect, it hadn't changed much over the years. Dead branches littered the rooftop, but the weathered logs framing the one-room structure still lent it a sturdy look.

"You still have that chain saw?"

Startled, she glanced at Cade. "You think the road's that bad?"

"It could be."

She sucked in a breath. If trees blocked the road, it would take forever to cross the mountain. And what if the fire came their way?

Determined not to panic, she hissed her breath back out. "It's in the toolshed." She parked between the trees behind the cabin and cut the engine.

Cade climbed down, and she opened her door to follow. Then she paused. She'd had a hard time cleaning that cabin, surrounded by impressions of Cade. Every chipped plate, every battered utensil had flooded her with memories, reminding her of those tender days. And the bed….

Her face flamed. No wonder she'd ignored the cabin all these years. It had been far easier to let it go than relive those delirious times. And how could she stand to be here with him now?

She had no choice. Steeling herself, she took a deep breath of pine-tinged air and stepped down. "We'll be right back," she told the dog and closed the door.

Fir needles cushioned her steps as she trailed Cade to the wooden toolshed behind the cabin. She tried not to walk too close, to keep some distance between them. She didn't want to feel his heat, his power, that mesmerizing tick of desire that consumed her whenever he was in sight.

He stopped at the door and waited for her to unlock it. She stepped beside him and that smoky scent reached her nostrils, along with the essence of Cade. Her head felt light, and her pulse quickened at the vivid memories. How many times had they done this together, coming home to the cabin? But back then, they'd be laughing. Cade would pull her close and nuzzle her neck….

Her hands shaking, her face burning, she fumbled to unlock the rusty padlock securing the door. She didn't dare look at Cade.

She finally unhooked the lock and stepped back. Cade moved forward and she braved a glance at his face. His jaw was rigid, the muscles along his cheeks tense.

Without warning, his gaze met hers. And for an instant, she saw that old fire in his eyes, the urgency and passion.

And then, just as fast, it was gone.

Unable to breathe, she yanked her gaze to the ground. And suddenly, an ache swelled in her heart, along with a deep sense of loss, as if something special had disappeared from her life, something unique. A connection, a sense of destiny she'd never felt with anyone since. And maybe never would again.

Her throat cramped as Cade shoved the creaking door open and stepped past her into the shed. His boots tramped hard on the wooden floor, and his wide shoulders filled the narrow doorway. She blinked back the blur in her eyes.

Seconds later, he turned and handed her a coil of nylon line with an old wooden clothespin stuck to it. Somehow the rope made her feel even worse, and the wedge in her throat grew thicker. It shouldn't have been fun washing their clothes by hand, stringing that line across the cabin in the winter, letting the clothes dry by the heat of the woodstove while they made love on the bed. But dear God, she'd adored this man.

She looked at his unyielding face and just then, it struck her. The deep bitterness he felt, the resentment. The fierce anger he'd fostered for years.

He blamed the collapse of their marriage on her.

But that was crazy! He was the one who had left. He'd chosen his job over her.

But he didn't see it that way. A sick feeling spiraled through her stomach. *Oh, God.* "Cade, I..." Her voice shook, and her heart battered hard against her rib cage. "Back there, when we were catching the dog, you said, you thought I'd...that I'd abandoned you."

He stilled, and the muscles along his jaw tensed. "You're trying to tell me you didn't?"

"Yes. I mean no, I didn't, I never..."

"Right." Bitterness seeped through his voice. "Well, you sure as hell fooled me." He made a sound of disgust and turned away.

And her heart balled even tighter. She never would have abandoned Cade. She'd loved him back then, truly loved him, with a passion bordering on desperation. He'd been the center of her world, the hero of her childhood dreams—or so she'd thought.

But even when he'd crushed those dreams, she'd never intended to hurt him. She'd just been too wrapped up in her own misery to do anything more than flee.

She gazed at his rigid back and her heart wrenched. She had to tell him that. Even if it didn't change how he felt, he needed to know the truth. He probably wouldn't listen to her now, and with the fire at their backs, this wasn't the time. But somehow, before they reached Missoula, she would explain.

He lifted a plastic fuel container with his left hand, shook it, and handed it back. Then he pulled the chain saw from the shelf. "When was the last time you used this?"

"I never have."

"Hell. The damn thing probably won't run." He set it on the ground outside the shed, turned back and grabbed an ax. He set that down next to the chain saw.

"That's it," he said, still sounding angry. "Let's go."

Her heart weighted, she tucked the clothesline under her arm, picked up the chain saw, and headed toward the Jeep. She heard Cade close the shed door behind her.

He helped load the tools through the rear window, and every jerk of his arm, every twist of his head tightened her nerves, reminding her of the unfinished business between them. Still, she was thankful for his silence. With her emotions so raw, she didn't trust herself to speak.

"The trail starts just past that boulder," he said when they'd climbed back into the Jeep.

"I remember," she managed. She pulled back onto the road and drove slowly toward the large rock, then stopped when she spotted the trail. Ferns sprawled over deep ruts and potholes. Branches poked through the clusters of weeds.

Her apprehension rose. "It looks pretty rough. Do you think the Jeep will make it?"

"It had better."

"You're right." No matter how primitive, this road was their only way out. She tentatively stepped on the gas.

The Jeep bumped over a branch. The grooves around Cade's mouth deepened and he cradled his arm to his chest. She hit the brakes, concerned. "Are you okay?" she asked.

"I'm fine."

"Are you sure? You don't look fine." His skin had paled and new creases lined his forehead.

He flicked his hard gaze to her. "Well, looks can be deceiving, can't they?"

A swift jab of hurt lanced her chest. "You think I deceived you?"

He raised a brow but didn't answer, and she yanked her gaze to the trail. So he thought she had deceived him, that she'd lied to him when she left. In a way, she didn't blame him. But he was wrong, and she had to explain that. She owed him that much after everything they'd shared.

But this wasn't the time. Her throat aching with guilt and apprehension, she pressed on the gas. Fortunately, dodging branches demanded concentration and she pushed the past to the back of her mind.

But that left her to deal with the present. And no matter how difficult the trail was, her senses locked on the man stretched beside her. His long, muscled legs and sturdy boots filled the periphery of her vision. Every time she inhaled, his low, smoky scent scored her lungs. Even the rasp of his breath stroked her nerves into heightened awareness.

But then, he'd always had that effect on her. From the moment they'd met, he'd taken command of her senses. The attraction had been instant, overwhelming, sparking a passion they couldn't contain. But even a fire that hot couldn't sustain a marriage, especially when Cade wouldn't stay home.

She glanced at him again and stifled a sigh. Unfortunately for her, the man still rattled her senses. Ten long years hadn't dimmed that attraction one bit.

Which was going to make this one uncomfortable drive.

About a mile past the cabin, the road started climbing. Thankful for the distraction, she stopped and shifted to all-wheel drive. The sun slid behind the mountain as she powered uphill, sending long shadows over their path. The pines turned a darker shade of green, and the warm air gradually cooled.

Suddenly, she spotted the old meadow and her heart

jammed in her throat. And despite her intentions, sensations clawed through her nerves, memories of rolling in that fragrant grass, alive and in love with Cade. When need had surged, and laughter had turned to breathtaking hunger.

Desperate to banish the memories, she stomped on the gas. The Jeep lurched forward, the meadow disappeared behind them, and she slowly released her breath.

She braved a glance at Cade. He stared straight ahead, the muscles along his jaw taut. Whether from pain or seeing the meadow, she didn't know. And no way was she going to ask.

A moment later, he cleared his throat. "Have you used this Liberty much off-road?"

She inched out her breath. "It's not mine. I rented it at the airport. I thought I might need an SUV if the roads were bad, and the Liberty was all they had."

His eyes met hers. "So you don't live around here?"

"No, I work in Virginia. I just came here on my vacation."

"To stay in the cabin?"

"No, to sell it." She pulled her gaze to the road. Frankly, she didn't know why he'd ever given her the place. She hadn't asked for it. And although she loved to hike, he was more the outdoorsman.

Maybe it had reminded him too much of her.

"So you don't come here much?" he persisted.

"No." Her gaze met his again. "This is my first trip back."

His blue eyes narrowed on hers. She waited for him to ask why she still owned a cabin she never used. Why she hadn't severed that tie to him years ago. Questions she'd refused to ask herself and certainly couldn't answer.

His eyes searched hers, and her pulse drummed in her throat. "Looks like you picked a bad time," he finally said.

"Yes." She dragged her gaze away. Her timing stank, all right, especially since she'd come back to get over him. And the irony of that struck her hard. Instead of being able to forget the man, she now had to spend hours trapped in this Jeep beside him, conscious of every movement he made.

Moments later, the trees on the side of the road thinned, and Cade straightened in his seat. "Stop for a minute, will you?"

"Sure." Anxious to put some distance between them, she braked and turned off the engine. Cool air blew through the open windows, along with the distant roar of the fire.

Cade grabbed his radio and climbed out. Jordan glanced back at the dog curled behind his seat and wondered if he needed a break. But what if she couldn't catch him?

"Sorry, sweetie," she said. "We'll let you out later, when we're farther away from the fire." She stroked his head, smiling when he looked up and whined. He really was a sweet dog. Thank goodness she'd found him in time.

She got out of the Jeep, closed the door and stretched to ease the tension from her shoulders. Then she joined Cade at the edge of the road.

She looked down at the forest and the air locked in

her throat. A sea of fire shimmered below them, rolling and seething like something alive. Brilliant orange flames streamed over the livid mass and whipped high into the sky.

"Looks like it jumped the road," Cade said. "It's a good thing we turned around."

She searched for signs of the road they'd traveled, but the fire had swallowed it up. She shivered, suddenly very glad Cade was with her. What would she have done on her own?

The cool wind gusted and blew her long hair forward. She gathered the thick mass and held it over her shoulder to keep it out of her eyes. "It's windy up here."

"It's that front pushing through." He lifted his radio and pushed a button. A small red light came on. "Campbell, this is McKenzie."

"McKenzie," Trey radioed back seconds later. "What the hell are you still doing out here? I thought you'd be soaking in a hot tub with some naked blonde by now."

Cade chuckled, and a swift pain cramped Jordan's chest. Caught off guard, she sucked in her breath. She couldn't be jealous. That was ridiculous. She and Cade were divorced!

She glanced at him, and her lungs closed up. He stood with his long legs braced apart, his wide shoulders framing his muscled body. Of course the women flocked to him. And when he looked at them with those eyes…

"Listen," he said into the radio. "We couldn't get through on the road, so we turned around. We're up on the ridge behind the cabin." He paused, and Trey said something she didn't catch. "It's pushing west," Cade said, "but the perimeter's erratic."

Her stomach still churning, she turned away. Below her, a tree exploded, launching deep-orange flames toward the sky. She tried to imagine people down there fighting that fire—smokejumpers like Trey and Cade. How on earth did they find the courage?

"You're probably going to need that tanker," Cade said. "The mud should help you get close. Just make damned sure you've got an escape route."

An escape route. She swallowed hard.

"Probably back inside the burned-out area," he added. "And heads up on this one. I don't like the way it looks."

Fear lodged deep in her throat, and she took a long look at the fire. She'd never understood that aspect of Cade—how he could stand the danger. It had seemed reckless to her, even selfish, that he'd risk his life for this job. Every time he'd left, she'd been terrified he wouldn't return.

And now that she could see the sheer enormity of the fire, the risk seemed even worse.

"Yeah, I'll keep you posted." He turned off the radio and his gaze met hers. And without warning, her world tilted even more. He was good at this, she realized, an expert. A leader who took charge and got the job done.

Not the thrill-seeker she'd once thought.

And he cared about his men. Enough to radio and help them, even when finding his own way out.

She cleared the sudden tightness from her throat. "Can they really put out this fire? It's so huge."

"It's getting there." He gazed down at the blaze.

"They'll have to get a tanker in here in the morning, probably bring in a hotshot crew and get more saws on the line."

"Why didn't they do that to begin with?"

"Because the fire wasn't big enough then." His gaze met hers. "Smokejumpers are the initial attack team. They drop us in while the fire's still small, and we put it out before it goes big." He smiled wryly. "At least that's the idea. If we can contain it, we save them a lot of money."

She looked out at the fire again. "You save more than money." That fire devoured trees and killed animals. And if it reached a populated area, they could lose homes and people, too.

She frowned. "I guess I never appreciated that before. I mean, I knew what you did, but I never really thought about the lives you save." She'd focused on the danger, the glamour, the excitement of leaping from planes.

The time he'd spent apart from her.

"You're a hero," she admitted.

"Hardly. I just do my job."

"You do far more than that. You're amazing." Their gazes locked. The seconds stretched. And she wondered if she'd really known him back then, ever seen beyond her own needs to the essence of this man.

And that bothered her. She'd come here to let go of the past, not to see Cade in a better light.

Or to find out she'd been wrong.

"We'd better go," he said.

"All right." Still unsettled, she followed him back to the Jeep and started the engine. He slid in the passenger side and closed the door.

"How far until we meet up with that Forest Service road?" she asked.

"Hold on. I'll check the map." He turned on the dome light and reached toward the backseat, then stopped.

The pallor of his face caught her attention. "I've got it." She grabbed the map and handed it to him.

"Thanks." He spread it awkwardly over his lap. After a moment, he lifted his head. "We should get to a river pretty quick. Once we cross that, we've got about twenty miles to go."

"Twenty miles? Just to reach a dirt road?" Her jaw sagged. This trip could take all night. And she couldn't imagine driving this trail in full darkness. "But what about your shoulder?"

"It's fine. I'm guessing my collarbone's cracked, that's all."

"That's all?" She gaped at him. "Are you joking? You must be in terrible pain."

"It's not that bad."

"Right." She didn't believe that for a second. "Is there something we can do?"

"We can rig a sling up later, when we're farther away from the fire. I don't want to take the time right now."

"All right," she said, still stunned. She knew they didn't have the luxury of stopping, at least not yet. "But let me know when you want to do it." She put the Jeep into gear and released the brake.

A quarter mile later, they crossed the ridge top and started down the opposite side. They descended slowly, working their way haltingly down the rutted road, every sway and jostle of the Jeep bringing their shoulders dangerously closer. Jordan focused on the path the headlights cut through the dusk, determined to ignore her nearness to Cade.

The smell of the fire finally faded, replaced by the strong smell of pine. She braved a glance at Cade. He'd fallen asleep, thank God. At least now he could escape the pain that injury must cause. And she could stop pretending he didn't affect her.

She let her gaze linger on his handsome face, on the hard, familiar planes of his cheekbones, the stubbled line of his jaw. The dim light emphasized the shadows under his eyes, his fatigue. He seemed vulnerable suddenly, exhausted, and she felt a reluctant surge of sympathy.

He'd always come home from fires worn out. He'd shower, wolf down more food than she'd thought possible and promptly crash into bed. And leave her feeling even lonelier than when he'd been gone.

She forced her gaze back to the road. After seeing that fire, she had to admit he had a right to be tired. She could only imagine the strength his job demanded.

Pensive now, she continued picking her way down the mountain. Soon she heard a low rushing sound over the noise of the motor. It grew steadily louder, and her hopes rose. They'd made it to the river. Now just twenty more miles until they reached a normal dirt road.

But then the headlights flashed on a barrier blocking their path and she quickly slammed on the brakes.

"What's wrong?" Cade asked, his voice rough with sleep.

She peered through the windshield at the metal pole. What on earth? "The road's closed."

He dragged a hand over his eyes and straightened. "I'll check it out."

"I'll come with you." Her anxiety rising, she pushed open her door. Why would anyone block off this old trail? Unless…

She hurried around the front of the Jeep. The sound of rushing water filled her ears. The Jeep's headlights shone past the barrier to the dark, swirling water below, and her breath jammed in her throat.

Someone had put up that pole for good reason. The bridge was gone.

Chapter 4

Cade strode around the roadblock and peered down at the river snaking through the rock-strewn valley. Months of drought had shrunk it back from its broad banks, exposing rocks and stranded deadfall. But even now, in this weakened state, it wouldn't be easy to cross.

"I can't believe this," Jordan said from beside him. "Why would anyone take out the bridge?"

Her voice floated to him in the dim light, and the low, throaty sound tightened his nerves. He forced himself to ignore that temptation and concentrate on the problem at hand. "The mining company probably built it. They wouldn't want to maintain it after they shut down. And nobody uses this road."

"Except for us."

"Yeah." Which was their bad luck, but he hadn't expected the trail to be problem-free. In fact, he was surprised they'd made it this far.

Jordan crossed her arms. "So now what? Should we turn around?"

He started to shake his head, but the stabbing pain stopped him cold. "Too dangerous. We need to keep going in case the fire turns."

"You think there's another bridge?"

"No, we'll just have to cross without one. The bank isn't steep," he added. "The Jeep can make it down."

Her eyes widened, and even in the low light he could see her alarm. "But what about the water? How do we get through that?"

He kept his gaze steady on hers, hoping she wouldn't panic. "I'm guessing it's pretty shallow with the drought we've had. But we won't know for sure until we're in it."

Her hand rose to her throat. He wished he could spare her this. He worked with danger and risked his life every day. But she'd always been more vulnerable, in need of protection. Or so he'd thought.

"If you want, we can leave the Jeep here and wade across," he said slowly. "I can come back later and pick it up."

"But then we'd have to hike to that road. And what if the fire turns? Wouldn't it be better if we had the Jeep?"

"Maybe." Depending on the path the fire took.

She turned toward the river again. The Jeep's high beams reflected off the thrashing water. The scent of moisture permeated the air. "I guess we'd better drive it across," she finally said. "But shouldn't we wait until morning?"

"More light won't help that much." The real danger lay under the water, with river rocks and mud. "And the way that front is moving, I'd rather cross tonight, at least get a firebreak between us and the fire." Even then, sparks could blow across, but he didn't mention that. She already looked anxious enough.

Her long sigh cut through the dusk. "All right, but you'd better drive. This is totally out of my league."

If only he could. He tried to lift his right arm, but sharp pain blazed through his shoulder, a deep, dizzying spasm that burned from his neck to his ribs. *Hell.* His damned arm was practically useless.

He clenched his jaw and sucked in his breath, willing the ache to subside. He'd always been the strong one, the man who took all the risks. Sure, he relied on his smokejumping bros, but that was part of the job.

But this weakness, this damned dependency…

His stomach balled, and something close to panic rocked his nerves. It was only temporary, for God's sake. He wasn't a permanent ground-pounder. He'd be back on the jump list in no time.

But it was still damned hard to admit. He forced his fist to uncurl. "You'll have to do it. I can't shift with my shoulder this bad."

The rushing water filled the stark silence. He felt Jordan's gaze on him, and his pulse slugged hard through his head, as if he'd just run the PT test. God, he hated being weak.

"All right," she said. "I'll try."

He flicked his gaze to hers, but didn't see condemnation. The knot slowly eased in his gut.

But then, she'd always had that effect on him. She'd been his oasis, his refuge, offering him the comfort and solace he'd craved.

"Do you want to make that sling now?" she asked.

"Later, after we cross the river. We can take a break on the other side."

Her eyes searched his. Her delicate brows wrinkled with worry, not for her own safety, but for his. His resentment slipped another notch.

And suddenly, he wanted to move closer, to feel that gentle warmth. To bask in her approval, her acceptance. *Her love.*

And that was as dangerous as the fire. He couldn't let down his defenses. This woman had the power to destroy him, just as she'd done before.

He'd barely survived it the first time. He'd spent months enraged, so bitter he could barely sleep. Always doubting, forever questioning, wondering what on earth he'd done wrong. And he'd be damned if he'd suffer through that hell again.

He yanked his mind to the river and stepped back. "We'd better go." Without waiting for her to answer, he circled the roadblock and strode to the back of the Jeep. Once there, he popped the rear window, picked up the nylon rope and tossed it on top of his PG bag.

A few seconds later, Jordan joined him. And despite his resolve, her soft, feminine scent invaded his space and heightened his senses. Annoyed by his reaction, he stepped away. "You'd better put a bag together," he told her. "In case we have to bail out midstream."

He heard her suck in her breath. He didn't want to

scare her, but they had to prepare. "I doubt you'll need it," he added.

"I know." But her hands trembled as she dumped out an athletic bag full of toiletries. She pulled a blanket and clothes from various bags, along with food from the cooler and a plastic bowl. "For the dog," she explained.

She zipped the bag closed and dropped it on the backseat. The dog raised his head and whined.

"Don't worry," she told him. "We're not going to leave you here."

She meant that, Cade knew. She would risk her own life before she abandoned that dog. Of course, he'd once thought she was that committed to him.

Shoving aside a rush of resentment, he closed the rear window, walked back to the passenger door and climbed in. Pain bolted down his shoulder with the movement. He panted quietly, sucking in fast, shallow breaths until the spasm passed, knowing this wasn't the time to be weak.

Jordan slid into the driver's seat and closed her door. She latched her seat belt, and her uncertain gaze met his.

"Ready?" he managed as the pain edged back to an ache.

"I guess so." Her gaze moved over his chest. "Do you want me to help with your seat belt?"

"No." He'd rather suffer than have her that close.

"This could get bumpy."

"I'll be fine. Let's just go."

"If you say so." Looking doubtful, she shoved the Jeep into gear, tightened her grip on the wheel and backed up.

"Try going down by that tree." He pointed to an alder tree still visible on the bank downstream.

"All right."

He gritted his teeth as the Jeep bumped over the rocky ground to the bank, which sloped gradually down to the river. The moon hadn't risen yet, but the headlights cut through the mounting darkness. The water gleamed as it floated past.

Jordan stopped and adjusted her hands on the wheel. Her knuckles shone in the dashboard's light and she inhaled sharply. "Here goes."

The Jeep tipped, and she quickly slammed on the brakes, throwing him forward. "I'm sorry!" she gasped as he hit the dashboard.

Pain stabbed his shoulder, and nausea flooded his gut. Stifling a groan, he shoved himself back in his seat. "Keep going."

She edged up her foot and they rushed ahead, bumped over a rock, then stopped. Feeling dazed, he sucked in his breath. "You're doing great," he ground out.

She slanted him a skeptical glance. "Sure, as long as you don't mind getting whiplash."

They sped forward again, dropped into a pothole, tipped to the side and jolted out. Struggling for balance, Cade braced his boot against the dashboard.

The Jeep lurched over another rock and stopped abruptly, ramming his knee to his chest. A spasm racked his shoulder and he fought down another groan. Forget whiplash. If she kept this up, he'd pass out before they reached the bottom.

But a few feet later, the bank mercifully flattened, and she let up on the brakes. The Jeep bounced down to the riverbed then stopped with a sudden jerk.

They both exhaled. A second later, her gaze met his. "Stage one. Now to get us through that water."

Cade's mouth curved up, and he felt a glimmer of pride, much like he did for his rookies. Despite her inexperience and fear, she'd pulled through.

"Any special route I should take?" she asked.

He turned his attention back to the river. The headlights lit the swirling current but the water beyond that was nearly black. "Not that I can tell. Get closer and we'll see how it looks."

"All right." Small stones and branches crunched under the tires as she drove forward. The Jeep jostled over the uneven ground, but didn't slip. When they reached the water, she braked.

He peered through the windshield. The water trickled harmlessly along the river's edges, skirting rocks and splitting into shallow side streams. But yards of dark, unbroken water stretched across the center.

"You think we can cross it?" she asked, her voice tight.

"We'll find out soon enough." His gaze met hers and he saw the anxiety crowding her eyes. "Hey." He lifted his hand to touch her, to stroke away the worry and soothe the rapid drum of her pulse. Then he stopped. She wasn't his to touch anymore.

He dropped his hand to his knee. "You'll do fine."

"Right." She managed a strained smile that didn't quite reach her eyes and flicked her gaze back to the river. Then she sat up straighter, eased out the clutch and drove in.

Cade stuck his head out the window to watch. The water barely moistened the hubcaps. "It's just a few inches deep."

"Should I go faster?"

"No, this is good."

The Jeep rolled steadily forward, swaying and bumping over rocks. The smell of water spread through the cooling night air. He glanced at Jordan and saw that she'd glued both hands to the wheel. "You're doing great."

"I don't know." She nibbled her lip. "I wish we didn't have so far to go."

"We'll get through it."

She shot him a quick glance. "You think so? It looks like it's getting deeper."

"Yeah." Ignoring his throbbing shoulder, he leaned out the window again. The water had inched to the top of the hubcaps. "But we're still okay." At least they hadn't sunk into mud.

They drove further into the river, and the water continued to rise. The Jeep tipped on a rock, and she righted it with a splash.

"Cade…"

"I know." He frowned at the water creeping toward the axle, then shifted his gaze to the shore. Hell. They weren't going to make it after all.

Resigned, he pulled his head back inside. "Okay, we'd better turn ar—"

A metallic screech rent the air, and the Jeep abruptly stopped. Oh, hell.

"What happened?" Jordan asked, her voice high. "What did we hit?"

"A rock, probably." Under the water where they couldn't see it.

"Oh, God."

He kept his tone calm. "It's all right. Let's try backing up and see if we can dislodge it."

She shoved the gearshift into Reverse and pressed on the gas. The tires spun, but the Jeep didn't move. She stopped, inhaled sharply, then tried again.

"Not too fast." He hung his head out the window as water streamed up the door. "Okay, a little harder."

She hit the gas and the engine's fan came on. "Not too much," he cautioned. She slowed, but then the engine sputtered and missed. "Stop!" He jerked his head back inside.

"What's wrong?" Jordan asked. The Jeep vibrated roughly, coughing and stumbling badly.

"Water probably got into the engine."

"Water? But how do we—"

The vehicle bucked, jolting them forward, then died.

The river's rush filled the sudden silence. Water splashed past in the light of the Jeep's high beams. "Try to start it," he said.

She cranked the engine. It churned and whined in the silence. She turned it off and tried again.

"You might as well stop," he finally said when it didn't catch. "We'll have to let it dry out."

"How long will that take?"

"Hard to say. A few hours maybe."

"A few hours!" Her gaze flew to his. "But we can't just sit here and wait."

"No." He kept his gaze steady on hers. "We need to keep going. We'll come back later and tow the Jeep."

She bit her lip as that shock registered, and tension

tightened her elegant jaw. But after several long seconds, she nodded. "So how do you want to do this?"

His respect for her rose. She was a fighter; he'd give her that much. Despite the setback, she didn't balk.

He returned his gaze to the river. "We can use the rope. We'll tie it off to the bumper."

"You think it's that deep?"

"Probably not, but the rocks could be slick. We'll hold on to it for balance."

"What about the dog?"

"He can swim."

"But what if he goes the wrong way? He might head back toward the fire."

He frowned back at the dog huddled behind his seat. The dog's worried gaze lifted to his. "I've still got that beef jerky in my bag. Won't he follow the smell of that?"

"Not if he's scared." She tapped her fingers on the steering wheel, her forehead wrinkled in concentration. "I can carry him across first, then come back and help with the bags."

The muscles along his jaw flexed. He wasn't that damn helpless. "I'll carry the bags. And if you're that worried about the dog, tie him to the other end of the rope. Then you can pull him along."

"That's a great idea." Her lips curved, and her blatant approval blocked the air in his lungs.

And without warning, the old dizziness seeped through his brain. That heady, off-kilter feeling that made him want to promise the moon. To do anything to feel her admiration, her respect.

Jordan grabbed her bag from the backseat and stuffed

her purse inside. Then she propped it between the seats and picked up the rope. "Are you going to take off your boots?"

Still feeling light-headed, he pulled his attention back to the problem at hand. "No, the rocks could be sharp."

"Then I'll keep my tennis shoes on." She handed him the rope, then pushed her seat farther back. Rising to one knee, she bent and lifted the dog. "You really do stink," she said as she slid with him into her seat. She kissed the top of his head and rubbed his ears. "But we're still not going to leave you."

She shot Cade a grin. "At least he'll get a bath out of this."

Impressed that she could joke under pressure, he shook his head. She was a trooper, all right. And that lethal combination of feminine warmth and grit made her hard to resist.

"Tie this to his collar." He handed her the end of the rope. "We'll hook the other end to the bumper and hold on to that."

"Got it." She threaded the rope under the dog's collar and secured the knot. Then she took a deep breath to gather her courage and pushed on her door. It didn't budge, so she shoved again, hard.

The door swung slowly open and she looked out. The dark, swirling water lapped at the floorboards, and dread spiked through her nerves. Good God, she didn't want to do this.

But Cade needed her help, and so did the dog. She sucked in her breath and hopped out. And shrieked.

"Cold?" Cade asked.

"No, it's great," she lied, shivering wildly. "Jump right in."

Cade's low chuckle drifted on the night air. She turned, set the dog back on her seat and grabbed the rope. "You stay here," she told the dog. Then she looked at Cade. He'd attached the headlamp to his hard hat and put it on.

"I'll tie the other end to the bumper," she said. "I'll come back for my bag and the dog."

Locking her jaw against the cold, she waded to the front of the Jeep. The icy water soaked through her lightweight sneakers and plastered her jeans to her calves.

Cade's door swung open, then closed. "You were right about the stones," she said as he came over. Even with her shoes on, she could feel them poking her feet.

She threaded the rope around the bumper and knotted it several times. She worked quickly, but her hands grew stiff from the cold. Cade switched on his headlamp for extra light.

"Let's see." He grabbed the rope near the knots and pulled. "Looks good."

A sense of victory spread through her, and she grinned. Maybe tying a few knots wasn't important, but at least she'd done something right.

Cade had both bags slung over his good shoulder. "Here," she said, reaching up. "I'll take mine."

"Never mind. I've got it."

"Don't be silly." Especially since he needed that arm for the rope.

"I said I've got it."

She recognized that stubborn tone. "Fine. I'll get the

dog." Her teeth chattering now, she waded slowly around her door to the seat.

"Here we go." She lifted the trembling dog, then paused to scratch his ear. "You know, you're pretty heavy for someone so skinny." Checking to making sure his rope didn't catch, she stepped back and closed the door.

Cade waited in the path of the headlights, the rest of the rope in his hand. "I'll go first," he said. He played out a few feet of line. "Hang on to this part behind me. And you might as well set down the dog. He can swim."

"In a minute." She clutched the shaking dog tighter and rubbed her cheek on his head. She didn't know who needed the comfort more, the dog or herself. "We'll get through this together," she whispered.

Cade waited until she grabbed the rope behind him, then started walking toward shore. She followed in his wake, letting the cold rope slide through her hand. The uneven rocks made it hard to stay upright and she tightened her grip on the dog. "We're okay," she said, more to herself than to him.

The current pushed against her knees as she waded along. She tried not to think about the dark, rushing water turning her feet to ice. She focused instead on Cade's strong back, relying on him to guide her.

Cade stopped a few yards later and waited for her to catch up. "You okay?"

"Yes." But she knew they'd freeze unless they picked up the pace. "I'd better put the dog down, though." She reluctantly set him in the water and tugged on the line, relieved when he paddled beside her. "Good boy!"

They started walking again. It was easier moving

without the dog in her arms, but the frigid water now crept up her thighs. She waded faster, forcing herself to breathe deeply despite the chills ravaging her body.

But God, it was cold. And the river was wider than she'd thought. For an eternity, she trudged behind Cade, slipping and splashing over the rocks, her teeth chattering nonstop. Then the water lapped her waist, and she gasped.

Cade stopped. "What's wrong?"

"Nothing." She locked her jaw to stop the clacking and shook her head.

He still looked at her. "You sure you're okay?"

"I'm f-f-fine. Just c-c-cold."

"Hell." He looked ahead at the bank. "We don't have too far to go."

But she knew she was slowing him down. He was already injured—badly, she suspected. He couldn't afford to get chilled.

But the river kept getting deeper. She glanced at the bags dangling from his muscled shoulder. The bags with all their dry clothes. "Are you sure I can't—"

"I've got them," he said, his voice hard. "Now get moving before you freeze."

He let go of the rope and hoisted the bags higher on his shoulder with his good hand. "You'll have to lead," he added. "I need to hold up the bags."

Too cold to argue, she plodded past him, then instantly slowed her pace. "Th-this is hard." With no one to guide her, she had to work to find the best footing, especially since a mistake could jeopardize Cade.

She stumbled, then quickly righted herself. It was definitely easier to rely on Cade, and not just to get through the river. She'd depended on him for so many things during their marriage. Companionship, friendship, love... Maybe she'd relied on him too much?

Jolted by that thought, she stopped.

"What's wrong?" he asked.

"N-n-nothing."

"Do you want to wear my hard hat?"

"I can s-s-see." She forced herself to continue walking. This wasn't the time to mull over their marriage. She needed to get them out of this river before they froze.

And God, it was cold. Shivers coursed through her body. Her teeth chattered so hard she couldn't think. She could only imagine how miserable Cade felt with his injuries.

She slipped and slid over a jumble of rocks, struggling to maintain her balance. The current pushed relentlessly against her, and she had to fight not to float downstream. But at least the dog had stayed with her. She tightened her grip on the makeshift leash.

Yards later, the rocks leveled out, making it easier to walk. But just as she started to relax, the rope ran out. She stopped.

"Forget the rope," Cade said from behind her. "We don't need it anymore."

She looked up in surprise. He was right. They'd almost crossed the river. And the water had dropped to her waist.

"You go ahead," she said. "I n-n-need to un-t-t-tie the dog."

"Forget it. We stay together."

"B-b-but—"

"Just hurry up."

Shaking, she pulled the dog into her arms, then struggled to untie the rope. Her stiff fingers couldn't work the wet knot.

"Take off his collar," Cade suggested.

She switched her attention to the buckle, but even that proved too much for her frozen hands. "I c-c-can't." Her desperation rose.

"There's a knife on my belt," he said. "In the sheath. Pull it out and cut the rope."

Shivering, she released the dog, and he treaded water beside her. Cade turned to give her access to his belt. Still shaking, she stuck her numb hand into the sheath and grasped the knife. Then she pulled it out.

And promptly dropped it.

Oh, God. She stared at the water in horror. It was too dark to see to the bottom. She lifted her stunned gaze to Cade.

"I'll get it," he said. "Here. Hold the bags for a minute."

She reached for the bags, then stopped. What was she doing? Cade was hurt. He shouldn't be getting wet. And what if he bumped his injured shoulder? She could search for the knife better than he could. Before he could stop her, she took a deep breath and plunged.

Completely submerged now, she groped blindly along the bottom with her hands. She felt rocks and silt, but not the knife. The current must have pushed it downstream. She rose, sucked in another breath of air, and sank back down.

This time, she swept the area a few feet away. She crawled along the rocks, running her hands over the bottom. Suddenly, the back of her hand brushed the knife. Relieved, she lunged forward and grabbed it, then stood.

Water sluiced over her face as she triumphantly brandished her prize. Cade took it from her shaking hand.

"Hold the rope so I can cut it," he said, sounding angry.

She clutched the dog's rope, and he sawed it off. "All right, let's go." He stuck the knife in his sheath and grabbed her arm.

Blinking back the water from her eyes, she started moving. But she could hardly feel her feet anymore, let alone keep pace with Cade. She stumbled, and he jerked her upright.

"The d-d-dog—"

"He's coming. Now hurry up." Cade picked up the pace and she couldn't turn back to check. Dazed, her body convulsing with shivers, she fought to keep up.

Seconds later, the water fell to her knees. Then suddenly, it was gone. Her teeth clacking hard now, she staggered across the dry rocks. Water squished through her shoes. The wind whipped her wet hair across her face, lashing her frozen skin.

The dog trotted beside her, then paused to shake. Relief swept through her. He'd survived.

She stopped, but Cade nudged her forward. "Keep moving. Over to those trees." He bumped her again, and she stumbled up the grassy bank to a cluster of pines.

"Stop," he said. "Now start taking off those wet clothes."

"The d-d-dog..."

"I'll get him." He dropped the bags to the ground, pulled out his radio and turned away.

Too numb to move, she watched him stride toward the river. A huge swell of emotion overcame her, cramping her chest. His shoulder had to ache unbearably. And he was wet, too; he had to feel terribly cold.

And yet, he'd carried their bags. He'd helped her to shore. And he still continued to work.

Not for her sake, at least not anymore. No, not because of her. In spite of her.

Because he was that kind of man.

The lump in her throat grew thicker, and feelings she couldn't name wadded her chest. "C-C-Cade," she stammered. He paused and looked back. "Thank you."

His gaze stayed on hers for an endless moment. The night stilled, and even her heart seemed to cease beating. Then he nodded and turned away.

Chapter 5

The cool wind tunneled through the narrow valley as Cade tramped back toward the stand of pines, the wet dog at his heels. He'd radioed dispatch to give them his position and get an update on the fire. Unfortunately, their news hadn't reassured him. The wind had increased and could switch directions at any time.

The wind gusted just then, creaking the pines overhead, and unease spread through his gut. Crossing the river had bought them some time, but they couldn't afford to linger. If the fire spread their way, sparks could blow across the river and torch the dry trees.

The dog stopped and shook, then trotted ahead of him to the cluster of pines. Jordan huddled in the windbreak, shivering in her wet clothes. Her dripping hair clung to her pale cheeks, and her lips trembled with cold.

He scowled. "Why didn't you change out of those clothes?"

She moved her mouth, then shook her head. Hell. She was colder than he'd thought. And no wonder. His gut still tensed at the thought of her diving into that river to get the knife.

Still swearing, he picked up their bags and dropped them at her feet. Unless he warmed her up, she'd never outrun that fire. But to do that, he had to get her into dry clothes.

Resigned to the delay, he dropped to one knee beside her bag. Using his good hand, he unzipped it, then pulled out a blanket and towel. Then he rummaged back through it again, this time netting a pair of socks, a T-shirt and jeans. And underwear. His hand clenched the strips of white lace, and he felt the blow to his gut.

So, she still wore that damn sexy underwear. Satin and lace, his biggest weakness. He dragged in an unsteady breath.

And forced his mind to focus on the problem at hand—getting her warmed up so they could escape the fire. Since she was too cold to move, he scooted over and lifted her foot to his lap. Still using one hand, he loosened the wet laces and pulled off her soaked shoe and sock. He did the same to the other.

He rose. "Now stand up so I can help take off those clothes."

"I c-c-can d-d-do…"

"No, you can't. Now stand up." Trying not to think of this sexually, he pulled her to her feet. He kept his mind carefully blank as he grabbed the hem of her wet shirt and pulled up. She crossed her arms to stop him.

"I could use some help here," he said.

"C-c-cold."

"Come on. It'll only be cold for a minute."

"K-k-kay." She straightened her arms, and he yanked the shirt over her head.

Despite his intentions, his gaze dropped to her full breasts straining against the wet bra. The moonlight shimmered on her delicate skin, darkening the valley between the soft swells.

"Turn around," he said, his voice hard. She pulled her wet hair from her shoulder and turned. But now her smooth, bare back gleamed before him, and without warning, memories crowded in, of undressing before the woodstove. Of sliding kisses down that delicate neck. Of cupping her soft, full breasts in his hands and making her moan....

He flicked open the clasp on her bra. She shrugged it off and crossed her arms, but not before the sight of her breasts seared his brain—the smooth curves shadowed in moonlight, the nipples tight with cold. The water beading on the firm flesh then trickling to her flat belly.

His pulse drumming, he grabbed the towel and draped it over her head. "Wipe your hair. It's dripping."

The blood surged hard in his brain as he picked up her dry clothes and faced her again. She dropped the towel and he slung the T-shirt over her head, struggling to get her arms in the sleeves.

He tried not to look at her swaying breasts, to focus

instead on the pain in his shoulder and the searing ache in his ribs. But hell, he was only human.

And she did have beautiful breasts. Full and lush, with creamy, pebbled nipples. Generous enough to fill his big hands.

And the memory of how those breasts felt in his palms came rushing back. Soft and slick. Arousing. Fighting the urge to touch her, he clenched his hand into a fist.

"We forgot the bra," he croaked.

"L...l...later." She pulled down her T-shirt, but the fabric clinging to her naked breasts did nothing to diminish his hunger. His mind banked down. His pulse ran ragged through his brain.

And he still had to take off her jeans.

Forcing air into his lungs, he moved closer and reached for the waistband. His hand shaking, he popped the snap and pulled down the zipper, and the electric sound tore through the night. Then he inched the wet pants down her legs.

He dropped to one knee, and she clutched his shoulder for balance. He welcomed the jolt of pain, especially since he was now eye-level with a scrap of soaked satin. Hardly breathing, he jerked the jeans off her legs.

He rose to his feet, her wet jeans balled in his hand. And God help him, but he couldn't pull off that underwear. Because if he reached for her, he wouldn't stop.

Knowing what she'd see if he met her gaze, he kept his eyes averted. "Can you manage?" he ground out.

"Yes."

Still not daring to look at her, he turned around, but

his ears stayed attuned to every movement. Every rustle brought visions to his mind, of memories he'd struggled to banish. His tension mounting, he picked up the dry lace and waited.

"Ok-kay." She stopped moving, and he dragged himself around. He tried not to look; he really did. But his gaze still fell to the thatch of dark hair between her thighs, down her long, slender legs and back up.

And it was his bad luck that his nerves leaped at the sight, and his body grew instantly hard.

She reached for the underwear, her hand shaking. He handed it over and turned away. He forced himself to look at the dog nosing around the trees. The moon rising through the thrashing pines. The river winding low on its banks.

"I'm d-done." He turned back, but the damn lace wasn't much better. His face rigid, he knelt and held open her jeans, but getting her inside them took forever. She balanced herself by holding on to his good shoulder, practically pulling his face in her lap. A sweat broke out on his brow.

He stood, and together they pulled up the jeans. He tried not to think about how close she was standing, about how with one short tug, he could haul her into his arms.

He jerked up the zipper and reached for the snap. His knuckles brushed her soft stomach and she gasped. Her gaze locked on his.

The air stalled in his lungs. She stood just inches away, her dark, sultry eyes hot on his. He smelled the velvet of her skin, the dampness of her hair, and felt the old urgency rise between them. His gaze dropped to her lips, and memories roared through his brain of staggering heat and pleasure.

The sound of the snap closing exploded like a bomb in the silence. He sucked in his breath and stepped back. Almost blindly, he bent and pulled his sweatshirt from his bag, then yanked it over her head. It reached her thighs, covering her like a sack. It didn't help.

He handed her the dry socks. "Can you put these on?" She nodded and lowered herself to the ground.

Struggling to control his libido, he again turned his back. So his desire for her hadn't faded. It didn't mean a damn thing, except that he was alive. Nothing had changed between them, or ever would. She couldn't live with a smokejumper. And he wouldn't change his identity for anyone, no matter how great their sex life had been.

His resolve hardening, he shoved the past where it belonged and turned his mind to what mattered—getting them out of the forest.

But the truth was that they couldn't continue in this condition. She needed to warm up. And although he hated to admit it, his head ached like hell. His shoulder felt wrenched from its socket, and his ribs burned whenever he breathed.

He picked up the blanket and draped it awkwardly over her shoulders. She gave him a grateful smile.

Keeping a safe distance between them, he sat down beside her and pulled off his hard hat. He took his canteen from his bag and rummaged for his bottle of ibuprofen, hoping to take the edge off his pain. When he found it, he thumbed off the plastic lid, tapped a few into his mouth, and swallowed them down with water.

He glanced at Jordan. "Are you hungry?"

Snuggled deep in the blanket now, she shook her head. His stomach rumbled, but food could wait. He needed to change out of his wet pants before he got chilled. Jordan wasn't in any condition to help him, and he doubted he could stand her soft hands on him if she were.

"We'll rest here for a while," he said. He began unlacing his boots.

"B-b-but the f-f-fire..."

"We're safe enough for now. We've got the river behind us and the wind's still pushing west. We can rest for an hour and then start hiking again."

"Your arm..."

"Later, when you've warmed up. You can help lace my boots up, too."

She looked at him for a long moment, as if she wanted to argue, then finally slanted her head. He tugged off his wet boots and socks.

He grabbed some dry clothes from his bag, then rose again. "I'm going to change." He turned his back to her and stepped away.

Using one hand, he stripped off his wet pants and briefs, and tossed them aside. The movement jostled his shoulder, but he ignored the deepening pain.

Then he picked up his dry briefs and paused. How was he going to manage this?

"You n-n-need help?" Jordan asked.

He froze. No way in hell was he was letting her help, especially after seeing her naked. He'd barely controlled his reaction to her then. "I can do it." Hoping she wasn't watching, he awkwardly inched the briefs into place.

His pants always hung loose during the season, thanks to the weight he dropped fighting fire, so he pulled them on without problems. He secured the zipper and button, and turned around. He'd have to go without the belt.

He sat back down and grabbed a pair of dry socks from his bag. "Any chance you can help with these?"

"Sure." Still wrapped in the blanket, she rose to her knees. Her hands trembled as she picked up his socks and unrolled them. He noticed her gaze didn't quite meet his.

He dusted the pine needles from the soles of his feet. "Are you any warmer?"

"A l-l-little." Her dark head bent over as she pulled the first sock over his foot.

He flinched. "Your hands are still cold."

"S-s-sorry." Still not meeting his gaze, she adjusted the sock.

"You can wear my gloves," he said. "They're dirty, but they might keep your hands warm."

"Okay." Her wet hair swung forward as she started on the other foot. He frowned. Aside from his hard hat, he didn't have anything to warm her head. And they couldn't risk building a campfire.

She finished pulling up his sock and sat back.

"Thanks," he said. "I'll put my boots on later." Maybe she'd be warm enough by then to help him lace them.

He tossed her his work gloves, then pulled more clothes from his bag to form a long pillow. He placed the radio close by, switching to the scanning position for updates.

Jordan settled back down beside him. "C-come here, sweetie," she called to the dog. He wandered over, and she patted the ground.

"We'll need to share the blanket to keep warm," Cade said.

"Ok-k-kay." She unwrapped the blanket. He scooted closer, and she helped smooth it over their legs. He couldn't hold her with his injured shoulder, but his body would still generate heat.

Stifling a groan, he lowered his back to the ground. He lay flat on the uneven surface, his right arm propped on his chest. His shoulder ached worse than when the tree had crushed it, and a dull pain pressed on his skull. He hoped to God the ibuprofen worked fast.

The dog paused a few yards from Jordan and began turning in little circles. After several rotations, he plopped down and buried his nose in his tail. Then he let out a sigh.

"G-g-good d-d-dog." She lay back and pulled the blanket to her chin.

Her concern for the stray dog touched him. He'd always admired that about her, that she really cared about others—animals, the elderly, even him. Or so he'd believed.

Shc shivered, and he moved closer so that their shoulders touched. The moonlight sifted through the pine trees and outlined the curve of her cheeks.

He forced his gaze away. His breathing slowed. And the fatigue he'd been fighting settled in, creeping through his heart and lowering his defenses. Rushing his mind back to the past.

God, he'd been crazy about this woman. She'd been everything he'd ever dreamed of. Gentle and tender. Warm and funny. Sexy as hell, with a passion that left him reeling.

And he'd been so sure he'd found the one woman who understood him, the one who really cared.

He'd been wrong.

But now, lying beside her and listening to her breathing softly, it was hard to hold on to the bitterness. Hard to forget the good parts of their marriage. The months in the cabin. The easy camaraderie. The trust.

He gazed up at the stars between the swaying treetops and listened to the rush of the river. And wondered for the hundredth time what had gone wrong, and why she'd left him.

His chest cramped, and for a terrible moment, he let himself relive the past. The incredulity. The disbelief. The bitter hurt and rage.

She'd hated being alone; he knew that. They'd moved from the cabin to Missoula during the fire season so she could find work and make friends.

But he'd never expected her to leave. He'd been stunned, shocked. Unable to believe that she'd gone, that something that special to him meant so little to her, and that she could toss it away. Or that he'd misjudged her so completely.

He closed his eyes and listened to her drift into sleep, just as he had years ago. So why had she left? A lost, lonely feeling weighted his heart.

Because even after all this time, he still didn't know the answer.

Jordan woke a short time later to sounds of Cade rustling through his bag. She snuggled deeper into the blanket, relishing the heat now spreading through her body, thanks to her dry clothes and Cade.

A sudden vision popped into her mind of him removing her clothes. Her shirt and bra, her pants… Her cheeks burned. Not that he'd had much choice. She'd been too cold to do it herself. But still…

Thankfully, he'd been all business—except for that one incredible moment when their eyes had met. Her heart fluttered wildly. She'd probably imagined that scorching look. Delirium induced by the cold.

But she hadn't imagined his naked backside. Her heart jerked, then careened off her rib cage. She hadn't intended to look, but his struggles had caught her attention. And then she couldn't tear her gaze away. The powerful lines of his legs, the solid muscles…

She swallowed hard. Cade was one gorgeous man. And at least she had finally warmed up!

Her nerves humming now, she moved her stiff body under the blanket. Fatigue weighted her muscles. She wanted to roll over and sleep until morning, but she knew they needed to go. That fire was dangerously close.

She forced herself to sit up. "Are we leaving now?"

He stilled, then continued rummaging in his bag. "In a minute."

His low voice rumbled through the night, and she shivered. God, she loved that voice, that deep, husky timbre that grew even rougher when they made love.

"You want some beef jerky?" he asked.

"Sure." Their gazes met, and his eyes, dark in the silvery moonlight, burned into hers. Her heart stopped. Oh, God. She hadn't imagined that look after all.

But then he turned his head, pulled a bag of jerky from his PG bag and set it down between them. "I've got some tuna and coffee we can have later, once we climb that next ridge."

She sucked air into her lungs. "I can make sandwiches, too." She removed Cade's leather work gloves, took a strip of jerky from the bag and tossed it to the dog. He grabbed it and trotted away.

And she fought to regain her composure. So she still felt attracted to Cade. And why shouldn't she be? He was a wildly exciting man.

Her heart fluttered. *Exciting* didn't begin to describe him. Her pulse drummed and leaped at the memories. That shocking hunger, the desperate need…

She bit off a piece of jerky, determined not to go down that treacherous trail. Thanks to Cade, she knew about thrilling men. The pleasure might be exquisite, but the price of that rapture was pain.

And she had to keep her priorities straight. She wanted stability when she married again, a man who came home every night. A man who cared more about her than his job. Not just passion, no matter how exhilarating it felt.

Determined to keep her mind on track, she finished the jerky and rose. She folded the blanket and stuffed it into her bag, then pulled out the plastic bowl. "Do you mind if I give some of your water to the dog?"

"Help yourself. You should probably drink some, too."

"I'm okay." She handed the bowl to Cade. He filled it and she set it down a few feet away. "Come on, sweetie," she called to the dog. When he trotted over, she smiled. "We need to give you a name."

She needed to get him on a leash, too. She couldn't risk him wandering off. But they'd cut off that rope in the river.

She eyed the belt Cade had tossed beside his bag. "Can I borrow your belt to make a leash for the dog? I can tic a sock to one end and hook it to his collar."

"Go ahead."

While the dog drank, she busied herself with the makeshift leash. The result wasn't pretty, but she thought it would hold. With that done, she collected her wet clothes and stuck them in her bag. Then she stepped from Cade's view to take care of necessities and put on a bra.

When she returned, Cade was tapping pills into his mouth. He chased them down with a swallow of water.

And suddenly, she felt guilty. He'd done so much for her, and she hadn't helped him one bit. "I can lace your boots now," she said.

"All right."

He rose to his feet in one movement, and she couldn't help but admire his strength. And his energy. He had to be more tired than she was, yet it didn't slow him down. Of course, his stamina had always impressed her….

He stepped into his wet lcather boots. Her face flaming, she knelt in front of him and began lacing. "Can you hold the pants out of the way?"

He pulled up his pant leg, and she secured the knot. "Is that tight enough?"

"Yeah."

She tugged his pants over the top of the high-topped boot, then started on the other. The smokejumping boots brought back other memories, of Cade replacing the laces and oiling the leather, her shock at learning how much they cost. "I hope the river didn't ruin your boots," she said.

"They'll be fine. They've been wet before."

She secured the second knot and stood. "How about that sling for your arm?"

"All right."

She grabbed the towel she'd used to dry her hair. "This is still damp, but it's probably long enough for a sling."

He slanted his head. "We need to bandage my collarbone first, to keep it in position."

"How do we do that?"

He knelt and pulled two long triangular pieces of cotton from his first aid kit. "Here. Roll these cravats lengthwise, then tie the ends together."

She knelt beside him and started rolling. "Like this?"

"Yeah, that's good."

When she'd rolled both pieces, she tied them together to form a long rope. "Now what?"

"Now we put it on." He rose. "But I need to take off this shirt."

She knew he had a T-shirt underneath, but the night air was still cool. "Won't you be cold?"

"Not once we start hiking. It's mostly uphill." He fumbled to undo the buttons with one hand.

She stood. "Here, let me." At five-nine, she was tall, but he topped her by a good six inches, even more with his lug-soled boots on. She reached up to unbutton his shirt.

The intimacy of the act made her face burn, and she kept her gaze averted. He'd completely undressed her, for goodness' sake. Surely she could take off his shirt without falling apart.

Gathering her composure, she undid the last button and gently peeled back the shirt. The biceps bulging beneath his short-sleeved T-shirt caught her off guard.

He'd always been strong, but years of wielding a chain saw had built real bulk.

But this wasn't the time to admire his muscles. She set his fire shirt on his PG bag, picked up the rolled cloth and cleared her throat. "Okay, what now?"

"Now you tie that around my chest to hold my shoulder in place. Make a figure eight."

"You'll have to kneel down so I can reach your shoulder."

He lowered himself to one knee, then helped her wind the cloth under one arm and over the other until they'd formed a figure eight. The resulting harness pulled his shoulder straight back. "How does that feel?"

"About right. Go ahead and tie it."

"So, how did you get hurt?" she asked as she fastened the ends together.

She thought at first he wouldn't answer, but then his head turned and his gaze met hers. "A snag fell—it was burning—and the rookie froze. So I pushed him out of the way."

She paused to picture that, and her heart skipped. "You saved his life."

He tilted his head, as if saving the man's life were nothing, and shifted his gaze away. And once again, she glimpsed that part of him she'd never acknowledged, even though she'd always sensed it was there. His enormous courage. His loyalty to his men. And she knew without a doubt that he'd do anything to help them, just as he had for her.

Except the one thing she'd asked him to do—stop smokejumping.

A tight feeling gathered in her chest. "So, the tree fell on you instead?"

"Not directly. The branches just glanced off my shoulder."

And nearly killed him, she suspected. "I see." Her throat thick, she lifted the towel and caught it under his arm. So he'd nearly died saving his buddy.

Their gazes met again, and for a moment, she was lost in those vibrant eyes. And she saw the need in him, the desire to save and protect. But who watched over him? Who helped him in return? Even a hero needed someone to lean on, someone to give him comfort.

Someone like her.

Seconds ticked by. She inhaled his masculine scent, felt the heat from his body rise.

And a yearning swelled inside her, a fierce desire to caress him. To soothe the tension in that hard jaw and ease his pain.

But he wasn't her husband anymore—because she'd left him. Feeling guilty, she straightened and pulled the ends of the towel to his shoulder. And felt the enormous strength of those muscles as she tied the knot on the sling.

He was tough, all right, and he was willing to bear the weight of the world. Including her.

But the one thing he'd asked in return—that she wait for him—was the only thing she couldn't do.

And she still needed to tell him why.

Feeling raw, she stepped away and grabbed the leash. "I guess we'd better go."

Chapter 6

The old mining road crisscrossed the mountain in a series of switchbacks as it inched its way toward the ridge. Cade led the way up the rocky trail, his headlamp carving a narrow path through the darkness. Breathing heavily, Jordan straggled a few yards behind him.

After listening to the chatter on the radio all night, he knew they needed to hurry. Come daybreak, the wind would kick up, and all hell would break loose on the mountain. He didn't want to be here when it did.

But Jordan couldn't hike any faster. He stopped and waited for her to catch up. Panting loudly, she staggered to a halt beside him, then braced her hands on her knees and gasped for air.

"How are you doing?" He clicked off his headlamp

to preserve the batteries, then blinked to adjust his eyes to thc moonlight.

"Fine." Still breathing hard, she straightened. "But I can't believe how steep this is. Every time the road turns, I think it'll level out, but it just keeps going up." She wiped the sweat from her face with her sleeve. "And I thought I was in shape."

He didn't want to think about her shape. He'd struggled to erase the image of her naked body from his mind all night. "At least we've got a road to follow. You should try hiking through the brush like we do on a packout. And that's with a hundred pounds on our backs."

"Your equipment weighs that much?"

"Usually more." He'd once lugged a hundred and twenty pounds for twelve miles over steep terrain. But at least he'd been wearing good boots. He glanced down at her canvas shoes. "How are your feet holding up?"

"They'll survive."

He hoped so. Hiking on these rocks with thin shoes had to hurt. "Are you thirsty?"

"Not yet." Her breathing still labored, she lifted her thick, wavy hair and bared her neck to the moonlight. Without warning, that image blazed hot in his mind, of her naked back, her long, slender legs, the provocative curve of breasts. His body went instantly hard.

Still connected to his makeshift leash, the dog lay down in the dirt beside her. Jordan let down her hair and bent to scratch him. "You're such a good dog," she cooed.

Her sultry voice plucked at his nerves. And more memories surfaced, of her whispering to him in the darkness. The heat as she moved against him. The feel of her soft lips on his.

She'd been an amazing lover. Sensual. Demanding. Hell, she'd been so damn hot that he still fantasized about her after all these years.

And that ticked him off. Scowling, he jerked his mind back to business—getting them off this mountain. He impatiently glanced at his watch. "The sun will come up in another hour. If you can last that long, we'll wait and eat then."

"I'm fine."

She straightened, and he eyed the bag on her shoulder. "I can carry that."

"That's okay. I've got it."

"It's just going to tire you out."

"Not that much. Besides, you're injured."

His stomach clenched at the reminder. Even after a handful of ibuprofen, his collarbone and ribs ached like hell—far more than they should for a minor injury. "A couple of lightweight bags won't do me in."

Her chin rose. "And I can do my part."

He studied the stubborn set to her jaw. Her feet had to be killing her, but she intended to pull her weight. And no matter what she'd done in the past, that determination impressed him.

"All right. Just let me know when you're tired." He clicked on his headlamp. "Are you ready?"

"Yes."

He continued hiking uphill, keeping his pace slow for her sake. She was a trooper, all right. But then, she'd always struck him that way.

Which had surprised him at first, considering how she'd grown up. The only child of a Coast Guard admiral, she'd lived in upscale communities in the nicest parts of the country, or in stately homes on base, whereas his family had eked out a hard-scrabble existence in the driest part of Montana, spending every cent they earned on the ranch.

And yet, despite her sheltered background, she had chipped right in, stacking wood and washing clothes at the cabin. She'd never made demands, never complained, at least not about the rough work.

The road switched back again, and he paused for her to catch up. "I'm fine," she wheezed, anticipating his question.

He checked his watch and glanced at the patch of sky visible through the trees. It still looked dark but most of the stars had disappeared. "It's almost sunrise. We'll look for a place to rest."

Knowing she was nearing her limit, he slowed his pace. A quarter mile later, he spotted a long, low boulder on the downhill side of the road overlooking the still-darkened valley. "This looks good."

"Great." Panting heavily, she staggered through the weeds to the boulder and sat. Still tethered to the leash, the dog plopped down in the grass beside her.

Cade followed and settled next to her on the rock. He swung the bags off his shoulder and handed her his canteen.

"Thanks." She dragged in another breath, then tipped her head back and drank.

He turned his attention to the valley below them. He

couldn't make out any shapes yet; in the predawn light, the trees blurred together in an inky smear. But in the east, a finger of fire crept into view. Deep orange and red, it shimmered in the fading darkness. He stared at it, mesmerized by the sight.

"The fire's beautiful, isn't it?" Jordan said.

"Yeah. It's something to watch." But it could turn deadly, especially when the winds whipped it up.

He shifted his gaze to the sky as the minutes passed, and watched it gradually brighten to blue. Smoke streaked the emerging horizon and mixed with the pink of dawn. Time ticked away, and the dense pines turned from black to dusky green.

And suddenly, he realized that it felt good sitting here in the forest, watching the sunrise with Jordan. They hadn't talked, hadn't needed to say one word. But even after all this time, being with her still felt right, like the natural place to be.

And no way was he analyzing why. He pulled out his radio and keyed the mike. "Campbell, this is McKenzie."

He waited patiently for an answer. After their all-night fight, the bros would be eating and drinking coffee, fueling up for the long day ahead.

Trey radioed back seconds later. "For God's sake, McKenzie. Are you still out here sloughing off while the rest of us do your work?"

"You call that work?" Cade scoffed. "Talk about slackers. A Girl Scout could have put out that fire hours ago."

Trey made another rude comment, and Cade laughed. Despite the banter, they both knew he'd give anything to be on that line instead of nursing an injured shoulder. "So what's the deal on this fire?" he finally asked.

"We've built a good line up the flanks, and so far it seems to be holding. But when that wind gusts up..."

"What's the forecast?"

"Just what you'd expect."

Cade's uneasiness grew. "They sending a plane to do a recon?"

"Yeah, it should be up at any time. We'll get some mud later, too."

"I'll be listening," Cade said. "And make damned sure everyone keeps one foot in the black." An escape route didn't do any good if no one reached it in time.

When Trey signed off, Cade radioed dispatch with his position and asked them to scout for a clearing. If there was any chance of a blowup, he wanted to get off this mountain fast.

That done, he stuck the radio back in his PG bag. "You want to eat now?" he asked Jordan.

"All right."

He slid off the rock and set his bag on the ground, then began pulling out food. Jordan knelt beside him. "I've got two cans of tuna, the beef jerky and instant coffee," he said.

She pushed up the sleeves of her sweatshirt and unzipped her bag. "And I have some strawberry yogurt, two oranges, part of a loaf of French bread and some Swiss cheese and salami I bought at a deli in Missoula."

He eyed their meager stockpile. Too bad he hadn't grabbed a couple of fire packs before he left the line.

That freeze-dried food would have come in handy. "I'm going to have some tuna," he decided. "You want the other can?"

She shook her head. Her hair was still damp, but dry wisps brushed her face. She tucked the loose strands behind her ear. "How long will it take us to get to that road?"

"At least another day. Maybe two."

"That long?" Small creases appeared on her forehead. "Then we'd better ration this out."

The tightness inside his chest eased. Rather than panic at their predicament, she was taking it in stride. Far better than he'd expected.

"Why don't we eat the perishables first?" she said. "I'll take the yogurt, and I'll make you a sandwich with the rest of this bread. It's already a couple of days old."

"Maybe half," he said. "We'll save the rest for later."

"All right." She repacked the remaining food in her bag and pulled out a plastic spoon. Then she took the bread from its plastic sleeve and split it in half.

While she made the sandwich, he took out his bottle of ibuprofen and downed more pills. Then he grabbed his map and climbed back up on the rock.

Jordan joined him a few seconds later and handed him the sandwich. "Thanks." He took a bite as she settled beside him. The dry bread was hard to chew, but he didn't care. By the time they reached Missoula, they would consider the stale bread a treat.

They worked silently through their breakfast, both too hungry to talk. Sparrows trilled in the pine-scented air. The valley brightened, despite the haze of smoke.

Far to the south, the mountains glinted in the rising sun, their jagged faces stark above the rugged land.

"I keep forgetting how far you can see out here," Jordan finally said. "It's amazing. And we're the only people for miles."

"Yeah. I've always liked that about my job, jumping into untamed forests." Wild, unspoiled places most people never saw.

Hell, he loved everything about smokejumping. The adrenaline surge when the siren blared. The rush when he leaped from the plane. The freedom of soaring through the air and the challenge of landing. He especially liked fighting the fire. Cranking up the chain saw and choking down smoke with the bros.

The job suited him in every way. And God help him, but he never wanted to do anything else.

He couldn't. Dread crept through his nerves, but he tamped it back. He wouldn't have to change jobs. Once his shoulder healed, he'd be back on the jump list, right where he belonged.

He finished all but a small piece of sandwich, which he tossed to the ground. The dog quickly wolfed it down.

Cade drank from the canteen, then handed it back to Jordan. "You'd better drink more water."

"How much do we have?"

"Enough for now. I've got two more canteens in my bag."

Her brow creased. "Can we give some to the dog?"

"Sure. We'll refill it at the next stream."

She tipped her head back and drank. The motion sent her hair tumbling over her shoulders, baring her long, slender neck to his gaze. His eyes followed the tempting curve of her throat to the swell of her breasts beneath the sweatshirt, then back to the moisture beading her lips.

He jerked his gaze back to the mountains and dragged in air. So ten years hadn't diminished her attraction. That was his bad luck, but he'd deal with it. He definitely wouldn't drop his defenses and let her close.

Careful to keep his gaze averted, he spread the map across his lap to get his bearings. He studied it for a moment, then lifted his gaze to the west. Along the slope of the neighboring mountain, he spotted a clearing, maybe big enough for a helicopter to land.

But to get there, they'd have to dip into the valley between the two peaks. And if the fire shifted and spread to that next mountain…

His gut tightened. They could never outrun flames rushing toward them uphill. On the other hand, if the fire jumped the river, they weren't any safer here.

"Are we still in any danger?" Jordan asked, as if reading his mind.

He couldn't lie, not when both their lives were at risk, but he didn't want to scare her. "We're fine for now. They'll send up a plane soon to recon the fire. If there's a place for a chopper to land, they'll let us know. We might not need to hike to that road."

She looked down at the valley. "But which way is the fire heading?"

"West, mostly."

"But it still could turn this way?"

"In this terrain, anything can happen." He folded the map and set it aside. "But we'll be all right."

Her gaze met his and she bit her lip. He saw her anxiety, her fear, and despite his vow to keep his distance, something moved in his chest.

"Hey," he murmured. He reached out and tucked a strand of hair behind her ear and his finger brushed her soft cheek. The early-morning sun cast a warm glow on her skin and played along the curve of her lips.

"Cade," she whispered.

"Yeah." He slid his hand to her throat, tracing the delicate line, then cupped the nape of her neck. The feel of her skin made his heart jerk. It felt right to tug her closer.

"I…I'm glad you're here."

Strangely enough, so was he. He lifted his gaze to hers. He saw the trust in her eyes, and something else. The awareness that always sizzled between them. The heat.

His blood thickened, and he dropped his gaze to her lips. Her full, moist lips. It had been so damn hot between them. Would it still be the same?

She swayed closer, and her warm breath mingled with his. Lured by the memory of that heat, he lowered his head.

The motion jolted his shoulder, and he froze. What was he doing? This was the woman who'd dumped him, who'd gutted his heart when she left. How in the hell could he kiss her? He dropped his hand and pulled back.

Disgusted with himself, he grabbed his map and climbed off the rock. Talk about a fool. How many times did he need to learn the same lesson? She didn't want a smokejumper. *She didn't want him.*

And he'd better get them out of this forest fast, before he forgot that fact.

He shoved his map into his bag. "You ready to go?" He didn't look in her direction.

"Do you mind if we check the dog's paw first? I want to see why he's limping."

"All right." Still angry at his loss of control, he rose to his feet and waited.

"Come here, sweetie," she called, tugging on the leash. "Come on." She climbed off the rock and stooped down. Her soft, sultry voice quickened his pulse and he swore silently. Why couldn't he ignore this woman when he knew she'd only cause pain?

The dog limped over, his tail slowly wagging. Still cooing, Jordan scratched his chin and scooted closer. Within seconds, she had him in her arms. "Okay, you silly dog. Let's see what's wrong with that paw."

Her eyes met his and her face turned pink, as if she were thinking about that near-kiss.

Reluctant to get near her, he dragged himself closer and dropped to one knee. They both leaned over the dog's paw, their heads nearly touching, and he inched himself back.

"I'm guessing he has a thorn stuck in it," she said and her blush deepened. "See if you can find it while I hold him still."

Forcing his attention to the dog, Cade reached out and clasped his paw. The dog instantly tried to jerk back. "Easy." He gently massaged the ragged pad until he felt something sharp in the flesh. "I found it." He pinched the thorn with his fingers and pulled it out. "Damn. No wonder he was limping." He held it up for her to see.

"Make sure there's not another one."

He tossed aside the thorn, then felt the rest of his paw. "I think that's it."

"Great." She kissed the dog's head and let him go. He scrambled away, and her gaze rose to his. "He must have run through brambles."

The concern in her soft eyes swamped him, and his head grew suddenly light. And that confused him. What was it about this woman that affected him so much? Why couldn't he keep her at a distance?

He forced himself to his feet. Needing to get away, to put some space between them, he strode to his gear and picked up his hard hat.

She rose more slowly. "So what do you think about Dusty?" She brushed the dirt off her jeans. "For the dog, I mean. I've been trying to think of a name."

Still annoyed with himself, but grateful for the change of subject, he shoved on his hard hat and lifted his bag. "I guess it suits him." Even after crossing the river, the mutt needed a bath.

"I think so, too. Come on, Dusty," she told the dog. "Let's get you a drink." She pulled the bowl from her bag and poured in water. While the dog drank, she stuck their trash in a plastic bag.

"You ready to go?" he asked.

"Yes." She put away the empty bowl, tied the trash to the strap on her bag and joined him on the path. "What kind of dogs did you have on your ranch?"

"Border collies, mostly. They helped herd the cattle."

"I could never have a dog when I was young. We moved too much." She hiked beside him up the rocky trail, her long legs keeping stride with his. “Plus, my dad was always gone on ships, and my mother couldn’t be bothered. She was involved with the wives’ club, and a dog didn’t fit her lifestyle.” She paused. “Actually, neither did a kid.”

The resentment in her voice surprised him. He’d always assumed she’d had a great childhood.

But now that he thought about it, she’d never discussed her past, at least not in any detail. Whenever he’d asked, she’d skirted his questions. And he’d never pursued it past that.

Troubled by that thought, he frowned. “How did you learn about dogs if you never had one?”

She glanced at the dog. No longer limping, he trotted easily beside her. “When I moved back East, I got involved in dog rescue. It helped me…cope.”

Cope? With what? Her guilt at deserting her husband? Bitterness soured his gut. “So you’re what, a dog trainer now?”

“Oh, no. Nothing like that. I still help out with rescue, but I work in a nursing home now. In fact, dogs are how I got my job.”

She stopped and pulled a pebble from her shoe. He waited for her to catch up. “I had the sweetest golden retriever for a while,” she said as they resumed hiking. “A trained therapy dog. Her owner had to give her up. So I took her to a nursing home to visit patients and got hooked.”

“Hooked on what?”

“The people.” She sounded surprised.

“Seems like they’d be depressing.”

"Not at all. I mean, when someone…passes on…it's really hard. But they're wonderful. They have the most amazing attitude. They know that they're going to…that they won't be around very long. And some are in a lot of pain. But instead of complaining or focusing on what they don't have, they're so cheerful and optimistic. They just enjoy every moment they have."

She frowned suddenly and nibbled her bottom lip. A second later, she slanted him a glance. He was surprised to see guilt in her eyes.

But then she cleared her throat. "Well, anyway, they're always happy to see me." Her voice dropped. "I guess I like feeling needed."

Needed? He stopped, feeling as if she'd kicked the air from his gut. "Since when?"

"Since when, what?" Her eyes searched his. "What do you mean?"

"You know damned well what I mean." He'd needed her, more than he'd needed to breathe. And she'd still bolted away. He turned and strode up the path.

"Cade, wait."

"For what? Another lie?"

"Cade, please. Let me explain."

His jaw rigid, he jerked around. "Explain what? Why you didn't give a damn about my feelings? Why you ran out of town?" He stepped forward and his gaze pinned hers. "Why your husband's needs didn't count?"

"But you… You didn't…" Her skin paled. "Cade, I…"

He waited, willing her to continue, to explain why she'd run away. But she only twisted her hands and looked distraught.

"Hell." Disgusted, he strode off. His gut churning, his pulse thundering through his skull, he struggled to control his anger. What did it matter? Their marriage was over. So why did he even care? Why did her betrayal eat at him, even after all these years?

Because he still didn't understand it. His heart pumping, he picked up his pace. Whenever he looked at her, whenever she talked, she seemed genuine. Sincere. As if she really cared about him. Hell, she even acted like that toward the dog.

And he fell for it, every damned time.

Was it just an act? Was she really that callous, that hard? And if so, why couldn't he see it? Why couldn't he get her out of his blood?

And if it wasn't a lie, if she really had cared about him, then why had she left? And why wouldn't she tell him now?

"McKenzie, this is dispatch," a voice on his radio called.

He pulled out his radio and sucked in his breath. No, he didn't understand it. But he did know one thing for damned sure. Before they reached Missoula, he was going to demand some answers.

Chapter 7

Jordan hurried up the rocky trail behind Cade, clutching the makeshift leash. A sick feeling swirled through her belly. She'd seen Cade in a lot of moods during their marriage, but never this fiercely bitter, and he had a cynical edge to his eyes that had never been there before.

Because she'd put it there when she left.

Fierce guilt cramped her chest. Of course he was angry. What had she expected? That he wouldn't care that she'd left him? That he'd shrug the divorce off?

Ahead of her, Cade said something into his radio, then shoved it into his bag. Then he stopped and looked back, waiting for her to catch up.

Her gaze met his as she closed the distance between them. His hard jaw tightened under the stubble, and his striking eyes narrowed at hers. And her heart tripped even more.

She'd hurt him, all right, deeply. More than she'd ever dreamed. And no matter how hard it was to discuss it, she owed him an explanation.

And she needed to do it now.

She caught up to him and stopped, trying to figure out how to begin. The dry wind swirled up dust and pushed a pinecone along the trail. The raucous squawk of a Steller's jay pierced the mounting silence.

She finally dragged in a steadying breath. "Cade, when you were growing up, was there anything you really wanted?"

He held her gaze for several seconds, and she thought he wouldn't answer. Then he turned and started walking again, and she hurried to match his long stride.

"Yeah," he said after a moment. "I wanted to get the hell off the ranch."

She blinked. "But I thought you liked Montana." In fact, she couldn't imagine him anywhere else. He was always doing something outdoors—hunting, fishing, smokejumping…

"Montana's fine. It was the ranch I hated. Doing the same damn work every day. Baling hay and feeding cattle." He grunted in disgust. "It was a hell of a life, being stuck in that dying town."

Still marveling over that revelation, she slanted him a glance. How come she hadn't known that? She knew the most intimate details of this man—what he ate, how he made love—and yet, in so many ways he remained a stranger.

Still, it made sense. Even injured, he exuded energy. She could imagine his restlessness as a teen. "So you were anxious to leave?"

"No way was I spending my life trapped on that ranch, worrying about the price of beef."

The bitterness in his tone caught her off guard. She studied the hard line of his jaw, sensing he'd had more at stake than a need for independence, but when he didn't elaborate, she let it go. "Well, I would have given anything to live there."

His eyes met hers again and he raised his brows. "You didn't like moving around?"

"Hardly." Her lips twisted. "Oh, some of it wasn't so bad. We lived in some beautiful places. But I hated starting over, being the new kid in school every year. Sitting by myself, trying to figure out how to fit in and what to wear. And just when I'd finally get it right, when I'd start to make friends and relax, we'd have to move."

"You can be lonely even living in one place."

"True." She glanced at him, wondering why she'd never viewed him as a loner. He'd always seemed so strong and confident, so impermeable to hurt. But apparently, she'd been wrong.

She gnawed her bottom lip, unable to stop the guilt creeping into her chest. If she hadn't seen that part of him, what else might she have missed?

"Well, anyway," she continued. "I didn't like to travel."

"How come you never told me that?"

Good question. "I didn't like to talk about it. It wasn't… It was a painful way to grow up. And I guess I assumed that you knew, that everyone understood the military lifestyle." Obviously, she'd been wrong. And that assumption had cost her.

The road switched back, and she paused to haul air into her lungs. Sunlight streamed through the Douglas firs in narrow beams, highlighting the punishing climb ahead. Cade held out his canteen, but she shook her head.

His Adam's apple dipped as he drank, and she steeled herself to go on. "My dad was always gone. That's how I remember my childhood, standing on piers, watching his ship disappear, knowing it would be forever before he came back.

"There was this one time when I was nine and he'd been gone for months. I'd been counting the days until he came home. I'd made one of those paper chains, you know, where you tear off a link every day? And the chain was finally gone."

They started walking again. "We got the call that the ship was in sight, so we drove down to the pier. We saw it in the distance, and then the pilot boat went out to meet it. I was so excited, I thought I was going to burst."

Her stomach clenched at the memory. And that old dread trickled in, that horrible sense of betrayal. "And then the ship stopped, right at the entrance to the harbor, and it started to turn. I thought that the pilot had told them to, so it could enter the harbor at a better angle, but they'd been called out on another case. They just turned around and left. I didn't even get to see him. And they were gone for another month."

Cade frowned. "Your father couldn't control that. He was just doing his job."

"Exactly. A job he cared more about than me." Her

throat tightened, and she searched his face, praying he would understand. "And that was my biggest wish growing up. To find a man who loved me enough to stay home."

She'd thought that man was Cade. He'd swept her away with his intensity, the way he'd made her the center of his thrilling world. And during those amazing months in the cabin, she'd lived the life she'd always dreamed.

Eventually, she'd discovered the truth, that she hadn't really enthralled him, or at least not for long. That he did everything with the same high energy, and he thrived on excitement and change.

And no matter what she did or how hard she tried to please him, she couldn't hold him down. Adventure lured him away every time.

Just as it had seduced her father.

Cade stopped and turned to face her. His eyes blazed, and a red stain inched up his neck. Shocked by his sudden anger, she took an unsteady step back.

He moved forward, crowding into her space. "So, because I didn't spend every damned second by your side, you figured I didn't care?"

Unease thumped through her chest. "It was worse than that," she said, her throat dry. "I hardly saw you."

"I stayed with you when I could."

"Sure, during the off season."

"During the summer, too. Every minute I wasn't working. What more did you expect?"

That he love her enough to stay with her.

"Is that how you measured our marriage?" he continued. "By how many minutes I punched on a god-damned time clock?"

"No, of course not, but—"

"Hell, you didn't want a man. You wanted a dog, somebody who'd sit at your feet every night." He jerked his head toward the leash. "Well, it looks like you got what you wanted." Looking furious, he turned and strode up the road.

Her face hot, her stomach balled, she slowly trailed him. Was Cade right? Had she expected too much from him? Had the problem really been her?

She dragged in a trembling breath. He made her sound so selfish. But was she wrong to want her husband around, to have a loving companion to warm the long nights?

She lifted her chin. "I don't think that's fair. Some men care more about their wives than their careers."

He turned back to face her, his jaw rigid. "It's not a matter of caring. A man has to support his family."

"By being gone all the time?"

"If that's his job."

She shook her head. "Not all men think that way."

He scoffed. "Good luck finding one who doesn't."

She looked away. "I already have."

"You're engaged?"

His incredulity stung. She snapped her eyes back to his. "Is that so hard to believe?"

His eyes narrowed even more. "What's hard to believe is that any *man* would stay on that tight a chain."

She flinched as he strode away. Phil was a man, a perfectly nice one. She pictured Phil's easy face, his laid-back smile. The warm brown eyes that were as comfortable and welcoming as her favorite armchair.

And about as exciting.

She scowled. All right, so maybe he wasn't as thrilling as Cade, but he'd make a great husband, wouldn't he?

Still frowning, she tugged on the leash and resumed walking. In any case, she wasn't looking for excitement this time. She wanted stability. She'd loved Cade passionately, but she'd been lonely without him. And it was far worse when she'd discovered she was pregnant.

Cade had been out on a fire, of course. And she had been so excited. She couldn't wait for him to come home so she could tell him the news. So they could celebrate. She was sure he'd quit smokejumping so they could raise their child together, and create the family she'd always desired.

But instead of coming home, he'd veered off to Alaska. He'd sounded cheerful when he'd called to tell her. Excited. Lightning was striking all over and he'd get plenty of overtime pay.

And she'd felt hollow, betrayed, as if she were nine years old again and that ship had turned around.

She'd started cramping that same night.

Her stomach curled at the memories. The shocking gush of blood. The panic and fear. The terror of lying alone in that starched white hospital bed, her husband a thousand miles away.

God, she'd been scared. She'd needed Cade desperately, and he'd been off fighting fires. And when she'd left the hospital, no longer pregnant, drowning in depression and grief, she simply couldn't go on. God forgive her, but she couldn't make herself go back to that empty apartment. She couldn't face the loneliness, the sadness. And so she'd left.

She sighed, unsure how to explain all that. How to tell Cade that he'd had a child, however briefly. And that she couldn't cope when it died.

Just then, a plane flew overhead, and she squinted up toward the sky. White wings flashed through the pines and then they were gone.

Cade waited for her to catch up. "That's the recon plane. They'll check for a landing spot, too. With any luck they'll pick us up soon."

Which meant their time together was nearly over. And she still hadn't told him about the baby. She cleared her throat. "Cade, I need to…"

Suddenly, a rabbit bounded across the road, flushed from the woods by the plane. It darted across their path in a fleeting zigzag, then disappeared through the trees.

A blur at her side caught her attention, and she turned her head to look. The dog bolted forward. The leash abruptly tightened and yanked her into the air.

Unable to catch her balance, she pitched forward. Her knee slammed into the ground, and she lost her grip on the leash. Gravel gouged her palms as she skidded along the road, and then her shoulder smacked the earth, knocking the wind from her lungs. She let out a muffled cry.

"Oh, hell." Cade ran over and crouched beside her. "Are you all right?"

She rolled to her side and groaned. "I'm fine. Just embarrassed." Of course, the dog would chase the rabbit. "I should have seen that coming. And I can't believe I dropped the leash."

Cade grabbed her arm and helped her to her feet. She rotated her aching shoulder. "I'm just bruised." But her knee throbbed. She glanced down and grimaced. "So much for my favorite jeans."

"Let's see." Cade squatted before her. Using his good hand, he parted the torn fabric. His finger stroked the periphery of the scrape, sending chills over her skin. "This doesn't look good. Can you walk?"

She bent her knee, felt the pain, and shook it off. "I'm fine." But her palms stung. She wiped them on her jeans.

He rose. "Let's see your hands."

"They're all right."

"Jordan…."

She sighed and held them out. Gravel and dirt were ground into the shredded skin.

Cade grasped one wrist to hold it steady. "Does it hurt?"

"No." She wasn't lying. The warmth of his strong hand had driven out any pain. And suddenly, all she could feel were the rough calluses on his fingers as he stroked her wrist, and the answering leap of her pulse.

He moved closer, bending his head to examine her hands, and her gaze traced his strong tanned neck, the blond stubble lining his jaw. He'd removed his hard hat, and his short hair gleamed in the light.

He looked up and scanned her face. "Looks like you hit pretty hard." He reached out and brushed her cheek. Her breath backed up as his fingers traced a path along her cheekbone, running thrills over her skin. Then he gently cupped her neck.

Her heart stopped.

His eyes narrowed, and he turned perfectly still. Tension arced between them. The familiar pulse of desire.

And suddenly, she wanted to kiss him, to feel that hard body lock against hers, those insatiable jolts of desire. To taste the bliss, the fire, even just for an instant.

And he wanted it, too. She saw the hunger in his eyes, the answering need. Her gaze fell to his mouth.

But he dropped his hand and stepped back. "We'd better get you cleaned up," he said, his voice strained. "I've got bandages in my first aid kit."

He turned away, and she hissed out her breath. What had just happened? Why had he stopped? She'd seen the desire in his eyes, just as she had on that rock.

It didn't matter, she reminded herself. She should be grateful that he'd drawn back. She had no business kissing Cade, no matter how exciting he was. That road led only to pain.

"Forget it," she said, determined to be as practical as he was. "We need to find Dusty first."

"After that trick? I'd say we let him go."

"Don't tempt me." He turned to face her, and she managed a shallow smile. "That was dumb on my part, though. I should have figured he'd chase the rabbit. I wasn't thinking." At least not about the dog.

And as a result, she'd lost him.

Cade pulled the canteen from his bag and strode back toward her. "Hold out your hands."

"I'd rather wait—"

"I got that part," he said, sounding impatient. "But at least we can rinse them off."

"They're not that bad."

"Humor me."

She sighed. Knowing it was useless to argue, she extended her hands.

He poured water on her palms, and the sting made her suck in her breath. "That's good." She pulled her hands back and shook off the water, then blotted her palms on her jeans.

"Let's see your knee."

She pulled a tissue from her pocket and held it out. "Just pour some water on this and I'll clean it off. I can do a better job later."

Cade dampened the tissue, and she quickly swiped at her knee. Blood oozed from the cut, but she didn't tell him that. She would wait and bandage it later, after they'd found Dusty.

Her apprehension rising, she stuffed the tissue in the trash bag. Then she scanned the forest, hoping for a glimpse of the dog. Dense pines blocked the view on the downhill side, while above them, a tall chain-link fence edged the road.

She blinked, amazed she hadn't noticed it before. Of course, her mind hadn't been on the scenery. "Where did that fence come from?"

"The mine." He stuck his canteen in his bag. "The entrance is probably ahead."

"What kind of mine do you think it is?"

"Could be anything." He picked up both bags and started walking. "Silver, coal, gold. Maybe vermiculite."

"What's that?" She limped beside him to keep up.

"A mineral they use in insulation. There used to be a big mine near Libby."

She absorbed that fact, impressed by how much he knew about these mountains. Of course, he'd grown up in the state and spent his spare time outdoors.

But that wouldn't help them find Dusty. Growing anxious, she whistled and scanned the woods. Surely the dog would come back. He knew they would feed him, protect him. Unless he ran too far and got lost....

A tight feeling spread through her chest. "Dusty!" she called, forcing back a surge of panic. She hadn't lost him. She couldn't have. She'd never forgive herself if that happened.

A few yards later, the road leveled out, and she stopped and gasped for breath. "We'd better wait here so he can find us."

"He'll catch up."

"Not if we're too far ahead."

Cade squinted in the sunlight. "Let's go up to that next bend. Then we can take a break."

"All right." Her knee aching, her palms burning, she reluctantly hobbled beside him. Locusts buzzed in the rising heat. The dry wind sucked at her skin. But at least the ground leveled off, allowing her pulse to slow back to normal.

Still worrying about the dog, she walked beside Cade to the bend, then turned the corner and stopped. To her surprise, boulders spilled over the road, blocking their path.

She wiped the sweat from her face with her sleeve. "What happened here?"

"I don't know." Taking the lead, he forged a path through the weeds around the boulders. "It looks like we can go this way."

She followed slowly. "Shouldn't we wait back here? The dog won't see us on the other side."

"That depends on where he is."

"I know, but—"

"Watch out." He stopped abruptly and held his good arm out to block her. She peered over his broad shoulder to see.

And gasped. Beyond them, the mountain had slid away. Instead of a dense stand of pines, huge rocks littered the hillside for hundreds of yards in either direction. Weathered logs were scattered throughout the debris.

She scanned the area in amazement. "My God. How did this happen?"

"Hard to say. Lightning could have burned some trees on the ridge and loosened the rocks. Or vibrations from the mine set it off." He glanced around. "Or maybe the mining company blasted the road to keep people out."

If so, they'd done a good job. She couldn't even tell where the road had been. "How are we going to get through?" Maybe she could scramble over the rocks, but Cade had an injured shoulder. And some of those boulders were huge.

"We'll have to go around."

She glanced up the mountain. Climbing the steep slope didn't look easy. And along the edges of the rock slide, where the earth remained intact, the chain-link fence blocked the way. "We'll have to go downhill."

"Too dangerous. We don't want to be below the rocks

if we set off another slide. This thing probably happened in sections." He nodded toward the nearest slope. "You see where that grass has taken hold? That's probably the original slide. But look over there." He pointed further out to a stretch of light-gray rocks. "That's more recent."

She nibbled her lip. Despite the danger, it would be faster to go straight across. "You don't think if we're careful…"

"It's too risky. The whole damn hill could collapse."

"Still…" A sudden yip caught her attention, and her pulse rose. "Do you hear that?"

"Yeah."

"Dusty!" she called, and another bark rang out. She edged closer to the slide and scanned the wreckage, sure the sound had come from there. But the only thing she could see was a hawk soaring past on the wind, trailing a shadow over the rocks.

"Dusty!" she shouted again. "Where are you?" Then she saw a movement and her heart leaped. "There he is!" The dog crouched between two boulders halfway across the slope. "We're coming, sweetie," she called out.

She turned to Cade. "His leash must be caught. I need to climb down there and get him."

"Forget it. The hill's unstable."

"But he can't get free by himself." Besides, this was her fault. If she'd held on to the leash, he wouldn't have gotten away.

And no matter what, she wouldn't leave him. Cade didn't know it, but saving dogs helped her deal with the loss of their child, as if by rescuing them, she could alter the past, or make it a little less painful.

"We'll have to go around and get him from the other side," Cade said.

"But that could take hours." The pitiful yips grew louder and tugged at her heart. She couldn't make him wait that long. She had to get him out now.

And only she could do it. The dog couldn't get free by himself, and Cade couldn't climb those rocks with his sling. Besides, she was lighter than Cade and less likely to set off a slide.

His eyes narrowed at hers. "Forget it," he said, as if reading her mind. "We're going around."

"McKenzie," a voice on his radio called.

"I mean it," he warned. He swung his PG bag from his good shoulder and pulled out his radio.

She moved closer to the edge of the slide. Cade didn't want her to cross because he was trying to protect her. But maybe she didn't need protecting. Maybe she was stronger than he thought.

She glanced back. He'd turned partly away, and she considered the breadth of his shoulders, the lean, muscled line of his legs. It had been easy to lean on Cade, to depend on his knowledge and strength. He was competent and brave, and it felt natural to let him take charge.

But maybe she'd depended on him too much, and that wasn't fair to him.

She swiveled her gaze back to the rocks. Surely she could do something as simple as rescuing the dog. It couldn't be that hard to manage. But she needed to move fast, before Cade guessed her intentions and stopped her.

She stepped onto the churned-up slope and immediately slipped on loose gravel.

"Damn it, Jordan!" Cade shouted. "Come back here."

"I can do this." Not daring to glance back, she regained her balance and threaded her way through the rocks.

Behind her, Cade swore, and she quickened her pace so he wouldn't catch her. She really could do this, no matter what he thought. She wasn't helpless—even if she'd once acted that way.

But soon the rocks jumbled together and she had to resort to climbing. She scaled one large rock, then another, and nearly reconsidered. The sharp stones bit through her thin-soled shoes. Her hands, scraped from her fall, tore more when she grabbed the rough rocks. And her battered knee protested with every step.

And even when she managed to find a level spot of ground between the rocks, the loose soil made it hard to stay upright. She slipped again, sending a stone crashing down the mountain and setting off a small slide.

Her heart pumped hard in her chest. Oh, God. No wonder Cade had warned her not to cross. But no matter what, she couldn't stop. Dusty depended on her to free him.

Her head low, she pushed aside her doubts and concentrated on inching closer, rock by grueling rock. Climbing up, then down. Sliding, skidding, struggling to stay on her feet, then scaling another boulder. And with every tortured step, the dog's frantic yips grew louder.

And she was getting hot. The sun beat down on her head and sweat trickled into her eyes. She blinked against the sting, then used the hem of her T-shirt to wipe her forehead. Blood stained the shirt where she'd touched it, and she wiped her raw palms on her jeans.

Breathing hard, she paused and glanced at the dog again. She was closer now and could see him straining to get free. "Hang on," she called out. "I'm almost there."

But she still had yards to go. With a sigh, she climbed up another rock. She refused to even think about the long trek back.

"Jordan, stop!" Cade suddenly called.

The urgency in his voice caught her attention and she glanced back. Cade stood yards above her, partway across the slope. "What are you doing?" she demanded. "I said I can get him. Go back."

"No! Don't move!"

"Me? You're the one who shouldn't be out here." Not with his injuries. Scowling, she found a foothold on the next rock and pulled herself up.

"Jordan, stop!" he shouted again.

Annoyed now, she paused and glared back. "For God's sake, Cade, I'm fine. Would you stop being so stubborn and—"

"Don't turn around! Jordan, please!" The panic in his voice made her freeze. She'd never heard that tone before.

"Good," he said, his voice tight. "Now straighten up real slow and raise your arms to look big. Don't let him sense that you're scared."

Scared? Of what? What did Cade see? Her nerves tightening, she turned herself slowly forward and scanned the rock slide. The sunlight glinted off the barren landscape. A puff of dust whirled into the air. The dog's desperate whines grew louder.

Then a movement slightly uphill caught her attention and she turned to look.

And gasped.

A big, tawny cat leaped silently toward her, his powerful muscles bunched under his fur. His ears pricked forward into stalking position, and his silver eyes locked on hers. A few yards above her, he paused, then lowered himself to a crouch.

Fear lodged deep in her throat, tightening the hairs along her nape and damming the breath in her lungs. A mountain lion. One of the fiercest predators in the forest.

And unless she stopped him, he was about to attack.

Chapter 8

His blood thundering, Cade scooped up a rock with his left hand and inched across the slope. Gravel slid under his boots, sending a stone bouncing downhill, and he froze. *Hell.* Unless he was careful, he'd spook the cat into attacking before he could get to Jordan.

He gauged the distance between them, and a sick feeling slid through his gut. He was still too far away to protect her. He had to get within throwing range so he could scare the animal off.

But he had to move quickly. A mountain lion could leap from twenty feet.

His heart ramming hard against his rib cage, he stuffed the stone in his pocket, then scooted silently over a boulder. He wished to hell she had listened to him. Why hadn't she stayed where she was safe?

And why hadn't he kept his eye on her? He'd suspected she'd go after that dog. Hadn't she plunged into the river for the knife? So why had he ignored his instincts and turned his back?

Regret speared his gut, along with a tight lump of dread. He'd screwed up, all right. He'd put her in danger, and now it was up to him to save her.

His gaze locked on the lethal cat, he inched closer. A vision of Jordan being mauled flashed through his mind, and a cold sweat beaded his brow. Damn his injured shoulder! Of all the times for his body to fail him. He wanted to leap over these rocks and rescue her now.

Schooling himself to patience, he scaled another boulder. But then Jordan bent to pick up a rock, and panic rocked his chest. "Don't bend down!" he urged her. "Stand up tall and look big."

She looked up at him, her dark eyes flashing with fear. "All right." Her voice trembled; her terror palpitated in the air.

And if he could sense it, so could the mountain lion.

Which meant that he had to move quickly. His pulse rocketing, he grabbed another stone and climbed closer. "Don't move," he urged her. "I'm almost there."

But then the dog whined again, the mountain lion crept forward, and Jordan threw her rock. It landed wide, and the big cat crouched again, ready to spring.

His heart stopped, and he hurled his rock at the cat. It hit near its paws and the cat looked up.

"Get out of here," he yelled. "Go on!" He whipped out the second stone and fired it, hitting the animal's side. The cat turned and leaped away, then stopped and circled back.

Breathing hard, he scooped up another rock and slung it. "Get out!" he shouted again.

Wishing to hell he could use his right arm, he hurled another stone. From the corner of his eye, he saw Jordan do the same. Her aim was off and the rock landed wide, but it kept the cat off balance. He thanked God she hadn't panicked and fled—because nothing triggered the instinct to pounce like running prey.

The mountain lion paced uncertainly for several seconds, then retreated a few yards and turned back. Cade flung another rock, hitting near its paw again. The cat hesitated a moment longer, then turned tail and loped through the trees.

Cade held up. Still breathing hard, he scooped up another rock and scanned the woods, poised in case it came back. Below him, Jordan rushed over the remaining boulders to the dog, pulled his leash loose, and gathered him into her arms.

"Hurry up," he called down, his blood pounding through his ears. Even though the mountain lion had left, he didn't plan to take chances.

"I'm coming." She set the dog down, wrapped the leash around her hand and started uphill.

His breathing rough, the adrenaline still rushing through his veins, Cade stood guard while she climbed toward him. Nothing moved along the edge of the woods, and a sparrow resumed chirping. When minutes had passed with no sign of the cat, he exhaled and dropped the stone.

He knew they'd been lucky. If that cat had decided to

fight… He blanched at the gruesome vision that thought conjured up. Jordan never would have survived it.

And he needed to get her off this mountain before that cat reconsidered and came back.

His emotions still churning, he worked his way across the slope, angling his path to intercept her. The midday sun simmered off the rocks, sending sweat trickling over his cheeks. The hot breeze swirled up choking dust and made it hard to breathe.

He kept a watchful eye on Jordan as she labored below him. The dog bounded easily up the slope, but she lagged behind, exhausted. And that ticked him off even more. What the hell was she thinking? She'd forded a river, hiked up a mountain and climbed through a rock slide, all on an hour of sleep. She'd had no business going after that dog.

He glanced down at her again, but just at that moment, she slipped. His nerves jerked and he lunged forward to help her, but he was too far away. She clutched desperately at a rock, missed and let out a cry. Then she started sliding downhill.

Oh, hell. "Jordan!" He lurched forward again, but the motion sent a stone crashing toward her, forcing him to stop. Any movement he made would only destabilize the hill.

He watched helplessly, a sick terror grinding through his gut, as the rocks surrounding her loosened and fell. The noise of stones colliding split the air, and she disappeared in a thick haze of dust.

Stark fear shot through his blood. "Jordan!" he shouted again, but his voice faded in the nerve-wrenching din.

Frustrated, he jammed his hand through his hair. He had to get down there. He had to help her! But how?

He waited an eternity for the noise to cease. Finally, a lone rock bounced down the mountain, and then the dust began to settle.

Seconds later, he saw her move. "I'm okay," she called out, her voice muffled.

She'd survived. He sagged and closed his eyes, then passed a shaking hand over his face. Good God, that was close. He'd never felt fear that raw in his life.

He watched as she awkwardly picked herself up from the dirt and checked the dog. She still had the damned leash clenched in her fist.

"We're both fine," she added with a little wave.

She rubbed the dog's face and murmured something. Then, after a quick glance downhill, she stepped forward. Even from a distance, he could see her wince.

He gritted his teeth. Like hell she was fine. A rock must have hit her. And judging by the way she was limping, she could hardly make it back up the hill.

With frustration gnawing his nerves, he paced a path in the dirt while he waited. Her face was pale, her features pinched as she climbed toward him. Pain carved a crease in her brow. And he'd never felt more useless in his life.

Then he noticed red splotches staining her shirt, and his lungs squeezed even tighter. She was bleeding. Just how injured was she?

He scanned the area, searching for options, and his sense of futility rose. Dense forest surrounded the rocks in every direction, leaving only the steep slope exposed.

A chopper couldn't land in these conditions. And even if it lowered a basket, the rotor wash could set off a slide.

Which meant they still had to hike to the road.

Suddenly, she let out a cry and stumbled again, and he instinctively lurched forward.

"False alarm," she called out. "We're all right."

All right? When she'd been battered by rocks? Outrage filled his gut. How could she sound so cheerful?

She paused to stroke the dog's ears, and suddenly he wanted to shake her. Damn that woman anyhow. Didn't she have any sense? To put herself in danger for a dog! Crossing an unstable slope, setting off a rock slide... And when she'd thrown that rock... His heart constricted with remembered fear.

And injured or not, it was time he laid down some rules. This was the last time she hared off on some damn escapade and nearly got herself killed. From now on, she listened to him.

Long minutes later, she finally staggered to his side. Her face was flushed, her breathing ragged. Exhaustion pulled at her face.

Unable to control his temper, he grabbed her arm and dragged her back to firm ground. The dog shook the dust from his fur and wagged his tail, unhurt.

Unlike Jordan.

"Damn it," he shouted. "Why didn't you listen to me?"

She shook her arm loose and frowned. "Because Dusty was stuck. He couldn't get away."

"You could have been killed. Don't you have any sense? That cat could have ripped you apart."

"But Cade, he—"

"He could have killed you." Why didn't she understand that? He couldn't have stopped him. He sucked in a shallow breath.

"And if I hadn't done anything, he would have killed the dog," she countered. Indignation flashed in her eyes. "What did you expect me to do? Just stand there and watch him die?"

"I expected you to follow orders."

"Orders?" A red stain crept up her cheeks. "You're not my boss."

"The hell I'm not." His temper flared even higher. "As long as we're on this mountain, I'm in charge. I know more about this forest than you do, and more about how to survive. So when I tell you to do something, you do it. And when I say not to, you'd damn well better listen."

"But Dusty—"

"Damn it, Jordan! Your life matters more than the dog's. Can't you understand that? You just about got yourself killed."

She bit her lip and looked away. He sucked in his breath and struggled to control his rage.

She met his gaze again, her dark eyes huge. "I'm sorry," she whispered.

His anger abruptly deflated. He dragged his hand through his hair. "God, Jordan."

"I'm really sorry," she said again. She stepped toward him, her chestnut eyes soft on his. "I didn't mean to scare you."

But she had. He couldn't even think about what might have happened. His throat clenched tight, and he shook his head.

"Cade, I..."

"Yeah." He swallowed, grappling with unnamed emotions, shocked at the depth of his fear. Why was he so scared? Sure, she'd nearly died, but so had the rookie when that snag fell. And he hadn't felt that gut-wrenching terror, that mind-numbing dread for the kid. Or lost his temper and yelled.

His gaze met hers again. A scrape marred her cheek beneath the dirt, and fatigue haunted her eyes. And suddenly, the need to touch her swamped him. The need to feel her, hold her, to prove that she was all right.

He closed the short distance between them. Then, hardly breathing, he lifted his hand to her face. He traced the scrape on her cheek with his thumb, felt the heat of her delicate skin. "You're hurt."

She shook her head. "Just bruised."

"You've got blood on your shirt."

"My hands got scraped, that's all. I'm fine, Cade. Really."

But she'd almost died. He'd almost lost her. *Again.*

His heart drumming, he slid his hand to her neck. He drew his thumb along her throat, and felt the strong, hot leap of her pulse.

Her breath hitched in the silence. Her pulse trembled under his hand. And as he gazed into those exotic eyes, feeling that inevitable pull, he knew that he had to kiss her.

Hardly breathing, he tilted her chin and lowered his head, then slid his lips over hers.

The years disappeared in an instant. The bitter memories faded away. Time peeled back and stalled on a glimpse of perfection. On Jordan, the woman he'd loved. And she was finally back in his arms.

Her soft lips parted, granting him access, and with a groan, he pulled her against him. He drank in her heat, her desire, the incredible feel of her skin, and explored her hot mouth with his tongue.

He felt her free hand clench his shoulder, then slowly rise to his neck. And then her tongue twined with his, matching his heat with her answering hunger.

But then she'd always been that way, fitting him perfectly, matching his needs, stoking the unending fire.

He plunged his hand through her hair and cradled her head, deepening and lengthening the kiss. His body grew hard. Raw hunger drummed through his veins.

And he had to face the harsh truth. No other woman had ever felt this good—or ever would.

Even if she didn't want him.

He jerked his head back and broke the kiss, then struggled to regain his sanity. This was wrong. Jordan had deserted him. And damned if he'd let her twist herself around his soul so she could do it again.

But her smoldering eyes locked on his, and she moved back into his arms. "Cade," she whispered. "Please don't stop."

And despite knowing better, despite the warnings rocking his brain, he knew he was going to give in. He still wanted her. Damn, but he still wanted her. And hell if he could resist.

With a groan, he lowered his head and slanted his mouth over hers. He heard her small cry, felt her welcome as she opened beneath him.

A sense of finality filled him. Of rightness. As if he'd met his destiny and arrived where he belonged.

Tightening his hold, he kissed her deeply, invading her mouth with his tongue. Trying to ease the ache, the need he'd refused to acknowledge for years. The need for Jordan.

But it only fanned even higher.

Her hand crept through his hair, and her soft breasts brushed his trapped arm. Desperate to feel her, he widened his stance and pulled her lower body against him.

And felt that urgency rip through him, that electric rush of desire. The need to bury himself deep inside her and forget the pain.

"McKenzie."

His blood thickened as he continued to kiss her. His mind blurred, while hunger twisted his gut.

"McKenzie."

Irritated, he lifted his head. His brain still fuzzy, his breathing rough, he scowled around at the rocks.

Jordan's eyes slowly opened and she blinked, looking as dazed as he felt. And as aroused. He wanted to haul her back into his arms. Even covered with grime, he'd never seen a more desirable woman.

"McKenzie," the voice called again.

His radio. He battled the urge to ignore it. He wanted to feel her hot, naked skin under his. To slake this wild need clawing his gut. To lose control and make love to Jordan.

Shocked at himself, he dropped his hand and stepped back. What in the hell was he thinking? She didn't want a smokejumper. She'd told him that point-blank. And no matter how strong the temptation, he refused to subject himself to that pain again.

Because this woman was different. They could never have an affair. Every time he touched her, he put his heart on the line.

Disgusted, he turned and strode to his PG bag. Even worse, that kiss had been unprofessional. A forest fire breathed up their backs. A mountain lion lurked nearby. They didn't have time to fool around.

Appalled by his behavior, he jerked his radio from the bag and keyed the mike. The red light flashed, and he swore. Great. This was all he needed. The batteries were low, and he didn't have any spares. He'd given his extras to Trey when he left the cabin.

"McKenzie here," he snapped.

"This is dispatch."

"Yeah." He shook his head to clear it. "What's up?"

"We checked out that clearing you saw, and think we can set down a chopper."

He pulled his mind back to the fire. They could hike to the clearing, as long as Jordan held up. But did they have enough time? "What's the fire doing?"

"It's making a run to the north right now."

Which meant it was heading straight toward them. He shot an uneasy gaze to the south, where the tall pines bobbed in his direction. If he hadn't been so distracted by Jordan, he would have noticed the change.

"How long do you expect this wind to hold?"

"At least until tonight," the dispatcher said. "We'll get an update in a few hours."

He thought hard. Alone, he could make that clearing

in five or six hours, less if he picked up the pace. But Jordan could barely hang on now. And unless she got some rest soon, she'd collapse.

And if the wind switched back before they got to that clearing, they'd be in a hell of a mess. The worst place they could possibly be was on a steep slope with fire burning below them.

But did they have a choice? At the rate they were traveling, it would take days to reach that road. And if the wind didn't shift, the fire would catch them right here.

He eyed the rock slide slowing their progress. "Any chance you can get a vehicle up this trail and meet us halfway?" That would shorten their hike.

"Hold on." While the dispatcher murmured in the background, Cade shifted his gaze to Jordan. She knelt in the dirt, examining the dog. Her eyes lifted to his, and he felt the kick to his gut.

He had it bad, all right. Just looking at her stirred up those old feelings, dredging up memories he'd rather forget. Making him want things he couldn't have.

Which was all the more reason to get the hell out of this forest.

"The road's blocked a few miles from the junction," the dispatcher told him. "Someone piled a wall of dirt across. We'll have to bring in a bulldozer to clear it out."

That wouldn't gain them any time. "Never mind. We'll get to that clearing. Just let me know if anything changes."

He lowered his radio and tapped it against his thigh. They were committed to that clearing now. He just hoped to God the wind didn't shift until they got there.

Chapter 9

Jordan stroked the dog's silky ears, her heart still fluttering madly from that kiss. God help her, but she couldn't stop reliving those amazing sensations—Cade's muscled body hard against hers, the exciting heat of his skin. The pleasure streaking through her nerves, turning need into desperation.

She dragged in a shaky breath. She had to get a grip. It was just a kiss, for goodness' sake. It wasn't that big a deal. Certainly no reason to act as though the earth had shifted.

She glanced at Cade as he stuffed his radio in his bag. Her gaze slid over the broad shoulders stretching the seams of his black T-shirt, the long, hard cords of his arms, the powerful thighs encased in dusty green pants, and down to his lug-soled boots.

And knew she was lying to herself. Cade's kiss had been anything but ordinary.

And if she'd learned anything from that miscarriage years ago, it was to face reality. She no longer hid behind the fantasies she'd clung to as a child.

And the truth was that she'd never reacted like that to Phil. Never. Kissing Phil had felt pleasant, comfortable, even mildly arousing.

But she'd never experienced that molten heat, that instant, carnal desire. That total insanity that, years ago, had made her elope with a man she'd just met—and even after all this time, even knowing the pain it would cause, tempted her to do it again.

Cade lifted their bags and stood in one smooth movement. He strode toward her, and another truth rocked her world. She'd thought she'd exaggerated her memories of Cade. That the passion she remembered was an illusion embellished with the passage of time.

But Cade's kiss had just blasted that theory. That passion was as real as this mountain. And it had nothing to do with her faulty memory. It had everything to do with this man.

She gave the dog a final scratch and rose. She struggled to compose herself as Cade drew closer, to act as if nothing had changed.

But then the seriousness of his expression caught her attention, and she shoved aside thoughts of the kiss. Something was wrong. Something to do with the fire. Alarm blazed through her nerves.

"What happened?" she asked.

His gaze met hers, and he stopped. The corners of his

eyes tensed, and her foreboding grew. "They can land a helicopter in that clearing the next mountain over," he said. "I told them we'd head there instead of the road."

"Why?" He wouldn't change directions without good reason.

"The wind shifted. We'll be safer heading that way."

Oh, God. The fire was coming straight at them. She jerked her gaze to the sky.

"We've got time," he continued, his voice even. "We'll take a break and eat before we start hiking."

Her gaze swiveled back to his. "But, if the fire's near—"

"It's not that close yet. We've got time to rest."

She opened her mouth to argue, but he turned and strode back toward the trail.

Still, doubts nagged at her as she followed him around the boulders and away from the rock slide. If they were fine, then why did he look so worried? And why wouldn't he share his concerns? What was he protecting her from?

She gnawed at her bottom lip. She was tempted to pretend she believed him and indulge in a much-needed break. Hunger drilled a hole in her stomach. Her knee ached from the fall in the road, her ankle throbbed where the rock had struck it, and blisters had chafed her heels raw.

And God, she was exhausted. Her head pounded like an off-balance washing machine, and even her leg muscles shook. She wanted desperately to curl up and sleep.

But she knew they needed to hurry. If Cade wanted off this mountain, the situation had to be bad. He wasn't the type to overreact.

And although he'd never admit it, this mess was completely her fault. She'd made them stop to rescue the dog. She'd gotten chilled in that river. She'd dropped the leash and spent the morning crawling across that rock slide.

Without her, Cade would be safe in Missoula right now.

Which meant it was up to her to keep them moving. She couldn't endanger him more.

A few yards down the path, he dropped their bags in a patch of grass. She hobbled to a stop behind him. "Cade, listen. I'm not that hungry. Why don't we take a break later?"

He swiveled around and faced her. "I'd rather eat now."

"But I don't think we—"

"And I told you we've got enough time." His blue eyes narrowed on hers. "Look, I wouldn't go that way if I didn't think that we could make it."

She scanned the hard line of his jaw, the implacable set to his shoulders, and realized she couldn't convince him. He was determined to protect her, even at his own expense.

She huffed out her breath. "Fine." So she would bolt down some food and act refreshed so they could get back on the trail. And then somehow, she would hike like a maniac to that clearing.

Cade lowered himself to the grass in front of a rock, his face tightening when he jostled his arm. Jordan joined him, careful to keep the dog between them, particularly with the memory of that kiss so fresh.

She pulled the remaining cheese and salami from her bag, then considered the orange. "How long will it take us to get there?"

"We'll make it by nightfall."

The finality in his voice plucked at her nerves. What happened if they hiked too slowly? She tightened her grip on the orange. "So we don't have to make this food last?"

"Probably not, but we'll save a can of tuna just in case." He pulled the other can from his PG bag, along with his canteen.

She scanned what remained of their food. "You want the rest of the sandwich?"

"Go ahead. I'll eat the tuna."

The distance in his voice made her frown. Was he that worried about the fire, or just determined to ignore the kiss?

Either way, she should be grateful. Better to treat it as a moment of insanity and forget it.

She reached over and popped the pull-top on the can of tuna. "Why don't I put the tuna on bread? It'll be easier for you to eat that way."

"All right." He leaned against the rock and closed his eyes. Fatigue hardened the planes of his face, along with deep lines of tension.

Just how close was that fire?

Her nerves drumming, she split the remaining bread into quarters. Glad to have an activity to distract her, she heaped the tuna on one piece and made a sandwich for Cade, then piled the cheese and salami on her own. Despite her intentions, her thoughts kept sliding from the fire to that kiss, and her nerves wound even higher.

She tossed the dog a chunk of salami. "Do you mind if I give Dusty your beef jerky?"

"Go ahead." He opened his eyes and took the sandwich. His gaze landed on the dog, and his expression turned thoughtful. "You know," he said, "that mutt was damned lucky. That cat could have torn him apart."

"I know." A spasm clenched her throat at the memory. She'd been terrified that she couldn't save him. And when that cat had prepared to leap…

Her hand trembling, she reached out to the dog and stroked the soft gray fur between his ears. His golden eyes lifted to hers, and she felt the tug to her heart. "It was close, wasn't it, Dusty?" Far too close. She never wanted to feel that fear again.

She gave him a final pat, filled his water bowl and fed him the jerky. Then she settled back against the rock to eat her sandwich. The stale bread had the texture of tree bark, but she devoured it anyway.

"Jordan." Cade's low tone pricked at her nerves. She met his gaze, and dread trickled into her gut. She'd never seen him look so serious.

"I meant what I said back there. It could get dangerous up on that mountain. Fire behavior can get extreme. And if it blows up, it happens fast. The conditions can change in seconds." His blue eyes stayed steady on hers. "So if I tell you to do something, I need to know that you'll listen. Even if it means leaving the dog."

She made an anguished sound. Leave the dog? And let him die? Her gaze fell to his furry face and her heart cramped even tighter. No way. She could never leave him behind.

Not even if it cost them their lives?

Her stomach balled in a surge of panic. Cade didn't know what he was asking. She pulled Dusty to her lap and hugged him, and buried her face in his fur. She couldn't fail this dog. He trusted her. He depended on her to get him to safety.

But she'd seen that blaze up close—the roiling smoke, the thundering flames. Fire streaming and exploding through trees.

"I'm serious," Cade said. "Our survival could depend on how fast we move."

Feeling shredded inside, she raised her gaze to his. And for an endless moment, she just looked at him, absorbing his strength and resolve.

And a deep sense of certainty filled her. No matter what had happened in their past or how he felt about her now, this man would do anything to protect her. She could trust him with her life.

She had to, because each time she'd ignored his directions, she'd caused more problems. So far, she'd only delayed them, and acquired some bruises and scrapes. Next time, she could get them both killed.

And no matter how wrenching it would be to leave the dog, she couldn't endanger Cade. "I understand," she whispered.

"Good."

She dragged her gaze back to the dog. But their situation would have to get extremely dire before she abandoned him. And she wouldn't let it reach that point. She'd hike like a demon to that clearing so they could outrun that fire.

Resolved now, she polished off the last of her sandwich and leaned back, pretending to rest. It wasn't hard. In fact, she had to fight the urge to sleep. The dry breeze swished through the weeds beside the trail, its hypnotic murmur sedating. Insects droned in the rising heat, lulling her into closing her eyes.

Determined to stay awake, she jerked her eyes back open. Then she brushed the dirt off her torn jeans and grimaced. God, she was filthy. What she wouldn't give for a shower and bed. A moan rose in her throat at the thought.

Cade reached for his canteen. "How's your shoulder?" she asked.

"Could be worse."

Or better, she suspected. He tapped several ibuprofen onto his thigh, tossed them into his mouth and chased them down with water. His Adam's apple dipped as he drank.

Her gaze slid down his whiskered throat, over the sinewy cords of his neck, to the makeshift sling cradling his arm. She felt a spurt of admiration. God, he was stoic. He had to feel worse than she did. He'd jumped from a plane, battled the fire and been crushed by a burning tree. Then he'd forded a river, tramped over the mountain, and stopped a predator from attacking. Yet he managed to keep himself going.

And if he could do it, so could she. "You ready to go?" she asked.

"In a minute." He passed her the canteen, then leaned back and closed his eyes.

"Mind if I take one of your pills?"

"Help yourself."

Deciding one wouldn't do, she shook three from the plastic vial and gulped them down. With a sigh, she recapped the canteen. Even warm, the water eased her dry throat. Now if she could only close her eyes… But she didn't dare. She'd fall asleep in seconds and not budge again for hours.

Unfortunately, that didn't give her much to do except look at Cade. Her gaze traveled over his familiar, handsome face. Dirt streaked his temples. A two-day growth of beard lined his lean jaw. Her pulse hummed. In all her life, she'd never seen a sexier man.

Without warning, he opened his eyes. His gaze seared into hers and her breath jammed. Her heart stilled, as if trapped by that heated stare, and she couldn't look away.

And the memory of that kiss swept through her. The frantic hunger, the clawing need. The pulsing surge of desire.

His hot eyes narrowed on hers. "So, who are you engaged to?" he asked.

Thrown by that question, she sucked in her breath. She couldn't lie to Cade, nor did she want to. They'd had too many misunderstandings in the past. They needed honesty now.

"No one, actually," she admitted. She lifted her hand. "Phil asked me. He's a guy I've dated for a couple of years, but I…I haven't made up my mind."

His gaze held hers for a long moment, but she couldn't read his expression. Then he stood. "Why not?"

Good question. Ignoring her protesting body, she rose to her feet and gathered their trash. "No reason. I guess I just needed time. He's a great guy. Steady, dependable."

Like a dog.

Their gazes latched. Cade's accusation hung in the

air between them. He lifted his brows, as if daring her to deny it.

Her face hot, she jerked her gaze away. She snatched up her bag and grabbed Dusty's leash, but questions crowded her mind.

Was Cade right? Was she expecting too much from a man? Was she wrong to want her husband to stay home?

Phil wouldn't think so. He never felt the need to roam, and he certainly never sought out risky adventures. His idea of a thrill was cramming in an extra round of golf before the evening sprinklers came on. And he'd gladly spend nights at her side.

But Phil had never kissed her like that.

"We need to head back down the road a half mile, then cut across the valley," Cade said. "We'll look for a game trail to follow."

"All right." Grateful for the change of subject, she quickly fell in beside him. But as she tramped along, trying to ignore her blisters and aches, she faced another harsh fact. If she married Phil, she'd never feel that excitement again. The only man who created that havoc was Cade.

And why was that? She loved Phil, didn't she? Frowning, she skirted a rut in the trail. Of course she loved him. Their relationship was just more mature, based on stability and respect.

Boredom?

Doubt slowed her steps. No, that wasn't true. Of course Phil didn't bore her. He relaxed her, sure, but wasn't that better than a roller-coaster relationship filled with extreme highs and lows? It was certainly easier on her nerves.

But if she loved Phil, then why did Cade affect her so strongly? Was it just lust? A heavy dose of sexual chemistry? Or something deeper?

That thought stopped her cold. Cade glanced back, and she hurried to catch up. Panic raced through her chest. She couldn't still love Cade. No, absolutely not. Loving him meant months of loneliness, reliving the misery of her childhood, being forever left behind.

Besides, she hardly knew him anymore. She'd changed since their divorce. She'd become more independent, more focused on reality, and Cade had probably changed, too.

She slid a glance at his rugged profile, and the cold truth slammed through her heart. Despite the passing years, he hadn't changed that much. He was still the amazing man she'd married. Generous and strong, brave and exciting—and unable to stay home every night.

Unless… Her breath hitched. Was there a chance he'd reconsider? That he'd give up his smokejumping job? Especially now that he was injured….

They reached the end of the mining fence, where the trail switched back and sloped downhill. She cleared her throat, not sure how to broach the delicate subject. "So, are your parents still living on their ranch?" she finally asked.

For a moment, he didn't answer. A Steller's jay squawked in the silence and the pine boughs creaked overhead.

Then he glanced at her, and she saw pain in his eyes. "They died in a car wreck a few years back. They hit a deer and ran off the road."

Oh, God. "I'm sorry. That must have been awful."

"Yeah." Tension carved grooves around his mouth, and he looked away. They hadn't been close; she knew that much. She'd met them once when they'd come to Missoula, and they'd seemed anxious to leave. But no matter how strained the relationship, losing a parent was hard.

Regret formed an ache in her chest. She wished she could have been there to help him, to comfort him in his grief. Knowing Cade, he'd shouldered the stark pain alone.

She reached out her hand to touch him, to let him know that she cared, but then she paused. He wouldn't welcome her solace, not anymore.

And strangely enough, that hurt. She dropped her hand to her side. "So who runs the ranch?"

"A neighbor. I sold it after they died."

Her heart dipped. "You didn't think that someday, I mean, after you'd smokejumped awhile, that you might want to go back?"

"I told you, I hated that place."

"I know, but..." She understood that when he was young, the ranch had made him feel trapped, but surely he'd matured since then. And he loved working outdoors. Why wouldn't he want his own land?

For several moments, neither spoke. They continued down the dusty trail, their long strides evenly matched. The dog trotted quietly beside them.

Finally, Cade slanted her a glance. "Look, you said that growing up, you had trouble fitting in."

"Yes." She sighed. "Maybe if I'd been more outgoing, it would have been different. But it was hard for me to make friends."

Which was why she resisted change now.

She blinked at that sudden insight. Was that true? Did she cling to security? Was she so afraid of rejection that she avoided doing anything new?

And was that why she'd chosen Phil? Out of convenience? She cringed. Good God, she'd turned into a coward. She'd nearly married a man she didn't love because he felt safe.

"I didn't fit in, either," Cade admitted.

Still shocked by her revelation, she forced her attention to Cade. "You mean on the ranch?"

"Anywhere," he said. "In school, in town. I felt like I was in prison. When I was a kid, I'd stand on Main Street, at the end where the highway started, just wanting to bust out so bad. To get on that highway and go. I thought I'd explode if I couldn't leave."

Her heart softened at the image of that restless, frustrated boy.

"But living on that ranch was pure hell," he continued. "It sucked the life right out of me. I wanted freedom, change. Something different to do every day instead of working that same patch of ground.

"No one understood that I was different." He shook his head. "Or maybe my old man did but he just didn't approve. Maybe that's what made him so angry—knowing I'd never come back, that he couldn't control me or make me live out his dream."

"Because you had your own dream to follow," she said, her throat thick.

"Yeah." He stopped in the rutted road. She paused beside him, and lifted her gaze to his. And saw the truth in those gorgeous blue eyes. The stark, unguarded truth. Straight down to the core of the man.

"Smokejumping's not just a job," he said. "It's everything to me. It's who I am."

Dread rolled through her belly. "But you can't do it forever."

"Close enough."

"Even if you're injured?"

His jaw turned rigid, his gaze hard. "I'm fine. My collarbone's cracked, that's all. It's not going to stop me for long."

"But…" She searched his eyes and saw his resolve. He was determined to keep on jumping. But desire alone couldn't make him invincible.

"I know you don't want to quit," she said carefully. "But what if you had to? What if something bad happened?"

"Then I'd join a hotshot crew and work from the ground, or learn to fly and drop retardant. I don't know. But I'd find some way to hang around this world. This is where I belong."

"I see." And, at last, she did. After a childhood of not fitting in, he'd found acceptance, respect, a place where he finally felt right.

A sick, sinking sensation pooled in her gut. And she understood something else now. He didn't jump for the adrenaline rush. He did it because he had to feel free—a feeling that was as vital to him as breathing.

A regular job would do more than bore him; it would crush his soul.

Which meant that the one thing she needed most—that he give up smokejumping—was exactly what he could never do.

Chapter 10

Jordan limped along the trail in the midday heat, reeling from her revelation about Cade. So he wasn't the thrill-seeker she'd thought. Her entire perception had been skewed—which meant that she'd misjudged this man badly. And now she had to rethink the past, their marriage, even herself in this new light.

And she might have to admit she'd been wrong.

Unease fluttered through her chest, but she ruthlessly tamped it down. No matter how uncomfortable she felt, she had to get at the truth. She had to peel back those protective layers and take a hard, frank look at the past—and her own role in it.

That was why she'd come to Montana. She'd expected to find validation, to prove she'd been right to leave Cade. Instead, she'd realized she didn't love Phil.

That kiss had blasted that illusion, cracking open the door on the truth.

And she couldn't shrink from the rest of it, even if she didn't like what she found out.

And a big part of facing that truth was telling Cade about the miscarriage. He deserved to know about his lost child. She never should have kept that secret.

Guilt blocked her throat at the thought.

"Hold up a minute." Cade stopped and glanced around. "I want to check the map."

"All right." She paused and shifted her weight from her tender ankle, then bent down to pet the dog. She'd behaved badly, all right. She'd fled Montana and ended their marriage, wounding the man she had loved. And when she told him why she left, she would hurt him even more.

Her throat thick, she brushed the dirt from Dusty's coat, and rubbed the soft fur on his head. He whined softly, gazing up with those trusting eyes, and tension slid from her heart. It wouldn't erase her guilt or change the past, but now she had a chance to do something right. She could finally tell Cade the whole truth.

But not here. Not with the fire this close. She'd wait until the danger had passed and he had time to listen.

Cade struggled to open his map, and she quickly rose to help him. "Here, let me get that." She grabbed the ends and held them steady.

"Thanks." His blond brows furrowed as he studied the map. Sunlight filtered through the whispering pines, highlighting the tips of his lashes. Darker bristles shadowed his jaw beneath his hard hat.

Her gaze caressed that rugged face and her pulse

began to hum. And that familiar ache came slinking back. She longed to touch him, to stroke that masculine jaw and see need flare in those dazzling blue eyes. To feel the power in those massive muscles and the rocketing thrills when he kissed her.

A gust of wind fluttered the map and snapped her back to reality. The forest fire. Their need to escape.

She sent an uneasy gaze to the south. She couldn't see the fire yet. The forest was calm, the patch of sky above the pines still blue.

But it was coming. She could sense it pulsing, seething as it roiled its way over the mountain. Thundering through the tinder-dry pines, devouring everything in its path—including them, if they didn't get out fast.

Her blood careened through her veins. Jittery now, she looked at Cade, and was startled by how calm he looked, how at ease in this dangerous world.

And for the first time, she realized she had a chance to see beyond the glamour to the reality of his job in a way she'd never had when they were married. To see who Cade really was.

And maybe, what she had lost.

He caught her gaze. "We'll cut across here on this game trail."

"That's a trail?" Surprised, she glanced at the faintly trampled grass leading into the trees, and her respect for him rose. "You certainly have an eye for details." She never would have noticed that path or survived out here on her own.

"It probably leads to a stream," he said. "We'll follow it as long as we can. But things could get rough after that."

"I can handle it." She folded the map and stuck it in the pocket of his PG bag.

He didn't answer, and she lifted her gaze to his. She saw the concern in his eyes, the worry. Not for his own safety, but for hers. He wanted to protect her, just as he always had.

Determined to do her part, she raised her chin. "I can keep up."

"Yeah." His voice gentled. "Just let me know if I'm going too fast or if you need to rest."

"I'll be fine." She'd make sure of it. She refused to slow them down, especially with their lives at stake. And she'd prove that he could depend on her, at least this time.

He dipped his head in agreement, then turned and hiked through the weeds. Intent on keeping up, she ignored her pulsating ankle. She focused instead on the power in his back, the impressive width of his shoulders, the confidence in his lengthy stride.

And couldn't help but marvel. God, he was strong. And not just physically. She couldn't imagine dealing with this terrible tension, this unbearable stress every day. Facing constant danger, taking risks, making decisions that could cost him his life.

"So, how did you decide to become a smokejumper?" she asked.

The game trail widened, enabling them to walk abreast, and he slowed for her to catch up. "I traveled around for awhile after high school. I worked in construction, did some logging, went up to Alaska and hired on with a fishing boat. But I didn't find anything that appealed to me long-term.

"Then, one summer, I joined up with a hotshot crew. I liked the work, the challenge of fighting wildfires. How every day was different.

"But it still didn't suit me. I needed more independence. Fewer rules. That's when I applied to smokejump."

She dodged a low-hanging branch. "You're saying smokejumpers don't have rules?"

"No, we've got plenty of rules. We don't fool around with our lives. But it's different. We're more like a group of individuals working together. We're all committed to the same thing, catching fire, and we can depend on our bros for our lives. But everyone thinks for himself. There isn't that obedience or regimentation."

She could see why that attracted him. Cade wouldn't obey anyone he didn't want to. He was far too independent.

And, to be honest, it was precisely that trait that had attracted her to him, his natural ability to lead.

And she'd followed him heart and soul. She'd leaned on him, depended on him, probably too much.

Uneasy with that thought, she frowned, but she had to admit it was true. He'd overwhelmed her back then. Not intentionally, but he'd been far too easy to cling to. And that hadn't been fair to him.

"The whole idea of smokejumping appealed to me," he continued. "Not only the work, but that so few people could make it. For the first time, I had a goal, something to work for. I'd never wanted anything that bad in my life. To be the best. One of the elite."

To belong.

She understood that now. He didn't jump for the

adrenaline rush as she'd once thought. Sure, he enjoyed that part; he was an intensely physical man. But he'd had a far deeper need, beyond the search for freedom. The need to prove his worth, to find acceptance.

And he had that now—esteem, admiration, the respect of his peers.

She eyed his steady stride and acknowledged the truth. Cade was an exceptional man.

And she'd tossed him aside. A sharp slash of regret tightened her chest.

"Hundreds apply every year," he added. "But only a few make it into the program. And some of those wash out of rookie training. Even former marines think it's tough."

Unsettled, she dragged her mind back to the conversation. "And even once you're in, you can't slack off." She'd learned that much at the cabin. "I remember how you worked out all winter to keep in shape."

His gaze met hers, and she knew he remembered that, too. "Yeah, we have to requalify every spring."

The path narrowed again, and she dropped back, ending the conversation. Grateful for the privacy, she gave in to her rising pain and let herself limp. Despite her assurances to Cade, throbbing heat bludgeoned her knee now, and she could barely put weight on her ankle. She longed to lie down and rest.

But if Cade could endure this trek with his injuries, she wouldn't let a few bruises slow her. Not when the stakes were this high.

The path wound through the trees as they trudged along, then dipped into a valley sheltered between the two mountains. The gentle murmur of pine boughs ceased, leaving an oppressive heat in its wake. The buzz of cicadas droned in the air.

But gradually, the stillness gave way to the rush of water, and the welcome scent of moisture. A few yards later, the trail ended at a shallow stream.

Cade crossed it in a few easy strides, then waited for her to catch up. She paused to let the dog lap the water and then gently tugged him across. Knowing Cade was watching, she struggled to hide her limp.

"How's your ankle?"

She grimaced. The man was far too observant. "Just bruised."

He raised a skeptical brow. "We'd better wrap it. I've got an elastic bandage in my bag."

"It's not that bad." And they couldn't afford to waste time.

"It'll get worse. Sit down on the grass and take off your shoe."

Annoyed, she propped her hands on her hips. He ignored his own more serious injuries, yet insisted on pampering hers. "It's really not that bad, Cade. I'd rather keep moving."

"Not until we deal with that ankle." His stubborn gaze drove into hers. "Look, I've had my share of twisted ankles. Smokejumpers land hard all the time. And the sooner we get that thing wrapped, the better chance we have of making that clearing."

"Fine." Frustrated, she plopped herself down in the grass. Phil would have listened to her. He would have kept on walking. But she couldn't push Cade around.

She tucked the leash under her hip to hold it in place

and started unlacing her damp shoe. Was that why she'd dated Phil? Because she could control him?

She mulled that over as she worked the laces. Phil certainly wasn't weak, but he didn't challenge her, either. Unlike Cade. When Cade decided something, he didn't budge.

She pulled off her shoe, wincing at the blisters covering her heels. Then she pulled up her pant leg and cringed. Her ankle had turned purple and swollen. And autocratic or not, Cade was right.

She sighed. "I guess I do need to wrap this."

He dropped the bags on the ground beside her, and lowered himself to one knee. "The elastic bandage should help." He pulled it from his bag and held it out. "Here, take off the clip."

While she pulled the small metal clip from the roll, he carefully lifted her foot. His warm, rough hand sent chills along her nerves. But then his thumb slid over her ankle and she flinched. "That hurts?"

"A little," she admitted, although she liked the feel of his hand on her skin.

He slowly rotated the discolored joint, and pain jolted up her leg. She sucked in her breath.

He didn't release his hold. "You need to get this X-rayed."

"I will. As soon as we get to Missoula."

His gaze met hers, and she saw determination in those vibrant blue eyes. "We'll make it out of here," he promised.

"I know."

He held her gaze, as if to convince her, and the years

suddenly peeled away. And for a moment, she was back in the time when he'd been the center of her world and dreams. When he'd been her fantasy man come to life. Back in the time when he'd loved her. Her heart fluttered deep in her chest.

But then he broke the gaze and gently propped her foot on his knee. "You'll have to help hold the bandage."

Shaken by the strong wave of longing, she hissed in a breath. "Okay, but don't put too much around my foot or I won't be able to get my shoe back on." She handed him the balled elastic.

He unrolled the end and draped it over her instep. "You'll have to hold this down."

Leaning forward, she pressed the elasticized cloth to her foot. Using his left hand, Cade carefully wrapped her ankle, passing her the roll to complete each rotation.

They worked together easily, a comfortable silence between them, the dog panting softly at their side. Behind them, the gurgling stream splashed past.

And without warning, she recalled another time they'd worked together, that Christmas when they'd decorated the tiny blue spruce. They'd passed the tinsel back and forth around the fragrant tree just like this, sharing promising smiles and molten glances. Until that inevitable passion flared and they'd started to kiss....

The dog nudged her arm, and she cleared her throat. "So, besides sprained ankles, what kind of injuries do smokejumpers get?"

He paused for a second, as if recalling old wounds, and then he slowly resumed wrapping. "Just what you'd expect," he said, his tone cautious now. "Bruises and cuts. Pulled muscles. Burns. Some long-term injuries. Knees take a lot of abuse, and the meniscus eventually tears. But usually nothing too grim."

Usually. She eyed the towel knotted over his shoulder and her nerves drummed. "But you *can* get hurt pretty bad?"

"Not often, but yeah. Guys get knocked unconscious and cut by chain saws, hit by rocks or worse." He stopped, and his gaze met hers. "Look, Jordan. You were right. This is a dangerous job. Parachutes malfunction. Fires blow up. And when something goes wrong, people can die."

Riveted by his gaze, she swallowed hard. "You never admitted that before." Any time she'd brought it up, he'd brushed aside her concerns.

"I guess when you're young, you feel invincible. You never think it will happen to you." He frowned. "Besides, I was your husband. I didn't want you worrying about my job."

So he'd tried to protect her. That made sense. Only she hadn't seen it that way.

She hadn't seen beyond her own fears to his courage, the fierce commitment to get the job done. To persevere and put out the fire, despite the personal risk.

Or to his need to shelter the woman he'd loved.

And suddenly, trapped in those piercing blue eyes, she felt a deep sense of loss. Cade was the most amazing man she'd ever met, and everything she'd ever wanted. But he wasn't hers anymore—and never could be with his lifestyle.

And yet, she'd loved him.

She still did.

Her heart stalled. It was true. She loved Cade. Despite the years, despite the divorce, her heart still belonged to this man. He drew her in and touched her in a way no one else ever could.

She saw awareness flash in his eyes and her pulse thrilled in response. So he felt it, too. That pull, that wild attraction, that insatiable, soul-wrenching need.

But what did that change? What did it matter? She jerked her gaze away.

And nearly wept at the awful irony. All these years, she'd wanted security. And when she'd finally found a steady man, one who would never leave her, she'd realized she couldn't marry without love.

And the one man she was destined to love, the one who touched her soul and stirred her heart, could never stay at her side.

He made a final wrap on the bandage, and propped her foot on his knee again. "Go ahead and secure it," he said.

Her throat cramping, a huge sense of loss weighting her chest, she worked the small metal clip through the elastic until it caught. "That's great. Thanks."

She managed to curve her lips up into a smile and shift away. Then, feeling shredded inside, she picked up her shoe, loosened the laces and worked it onto her foot.

While she tied her shoe, Cade collected their bags and refilled the canteens. Then she grabbed the leash and stood, allowing her weight to shift to her foot. The bandage felt tight, but it braced her ankle. She just hoped it would get her to that clearing.

"How does it feel?" Cade asked.

"Great."

"Jordan...."

"I'm fine. Really." Except she loved a man she couldn't marry. Ignoring the despair filling her chest, she forced her gaze to his. "Shall we go?"

"Yeah." His brows furrowed, and he looked troubled, as if he wanted to say more. But then he turned away. She waited until he started walking before she slowly fell in behind him.

A deep sense of futility filled her, but she shook the sensation off. She couldn't dwell on what she'd lost, not now. And she couldn't think about the future, or what could never be. She'd just concentrate on the present, getting herself up that next mountain.

No matter how much she ached for this man.

As Cade had predicted, the game trail had stopped at the creek. She let him take the lead, content to plod behind him as he blazed a path through the brush. She skirted huckleberry bushes laden with berries, detoured around alder and fir trees and crawled over decaying logs. Maneuvering through the rough terrain took concentration, giving her a welcome excuse to stay silent. The last thing she wanted to do was discuss her heartbreak with Cade.

But as the yards passed the slope grew even steeper, and her pace dramatically slowed. Her lungs burned, her breathing grew harsh and her chest felt stuffed with cotton. And despite the bandage, her ankle screamed with every step.

"Are you okay?" Cade called back.

"I'm fine," she wheezed out. A sharp branch scratched her face, and she batted it back.

So this was how Cade spent his summers, she marveled. Hiking through the untamed forest, going without showers for days. She wondered how he could stand it. She'd never survive a packout, especially with a hundred pounds of tools on her back.

Smokejumpers were a special breed, all right. She couldn't imagine competing for this job.

Exhausted now, she glanced at the dog. He trotted happily beside her, sending a slither of warmth to her heart. He looked silly with Cade's sock knotted on his collar, and despite crossing the river, he still desperately needed a bath. But at least he wasn't wandering through the forest alone anymore.

A few yards later, Cade stopped. Desperate for the break, she stumbled to a halt beside him.

"You thirsty?" he asked.

She sawed air through her burning lungs and nodded. He turned to give her access to his PG bag, and she gratefully grabbed the canteen. She drank deeply, greedily, relishing the moisture on her raw throat. She paused, wiped the sweat from her forehead with her sleeve and guzzled down more.

With her thirst partially quenched, she handed him the canteen. He took several long gulps and gave it back. She drank again, then recapped it and slipped it into his bag, ready to go.

But he didn't move. Still panting, she looked up.

"Why didn't you sell the cabin before now?" he asked.

Her breath stopped, and all at once she felt dizzy, as

if she hadn't the strength to stand up. It was a good question, one she'd refused to answer for years. And one she'd prayed he wouldn't ask.

But she'd dodged the truth long enough. She inhaled sharply to gather her courage, then locked her gaze on his. "I don't know," she admitted. "I guess I didn't want to think about it at first, the cabin, the divorce." *The baby.* "I hadn't expected you to give it to me, you know. So I didn't really know what to do."

"Your lawyer demanded the cabin in the settlement."

"I…I didn't know. I should have. I'm sorry." She swallowed hard. "I know that's not an excuse. I was young and silly. A coward," she admitted. She'd been so intent on avoiding Cade that she hadn't even questioned the terms. "I just wanted to forget.

"But it didn't work," she whispered. "I couldn't forget. Not the marriage, and certainly not you."

She searched his eyes, hoping he'd understand, but his expression remained blank.

She sighed. "Later on, I thought about selling, but I still couldn't make myself do it." She couldn't sever that last tie to Cade. "And I think… I knew that I had to come back here to face the past. To think about what had happened. But I didn't have the courage until now."

His hard jaw tightened beneath the bristles, and the muscles in his taut cheeks tensed. Then something like regret flashed in his eyes, along with the deep pain she'd caused.

Her heart made a slow, guilty roll through her chest. She'd never meant to hurt Cade. Never. She'd just been so racked with grief herself that she hadn't thought her actions through.

"Cade," she pleaded. She reached out to touch him. "I—"

He jerked back, stopping her cold.

Her throat thick, she dropped her hand to her side. "I'm sorry. I wish… I wish we'd talked like this before."

But they'd fallen for each other too fast. They hadn't given their relationship time, hadn't talked about who they were or what they wanted. Maybe she'd been too young even to know.

Instead, they'd communicated with their bodies and hearts.

"We both saw what we wanted to," he said, his voice quiet. "An illusion."

Dread chugged through her belly. "And what was it you wanted to see?" she whispered.

"A woman who understood me. One who loved me enough to wait."

The woman she could never be.

His jaw rigid, he strode away.

Chapter 11

He'd done it again.

His jaw clenched, his gut churning, Cade strode through the trees up the mountain. What was wrong with him? Why couldn't he control himself around Jordan? He should forget their damn marriage and keep it locked in the past. Instead, he kept trying to get closer, probe deeper, to figure out why she'd left.

As if he didn't already know.

Pinecones crunched under his boots. Low branches scratched his face, and he shoved them aside with a scowl. He knew the truth, all right, but he couldn't shake off the sensation that there was something he still couldn't see, something she had kept hidden. Some detail that would help it make sense.

Right. Talk about fantasies. Disgusted, he swatted

away another branch. He was pathetic around that woman, like some crazy lemming blinding himself to reality to hurl himself off a cliff.

It was those eyes that undid him. Those hypnotic eyes of hers pulled at him, sucking him under, making him want to ignore the truth. Convincing him she was the woman he'd once believed.

He hissed out his breath and glanced back. Her face flushed, Jordan struggled through the dense brush behind him. Devil's club arched close to her head, its flat leaves trembling as she pushed past.

And as he watched her climb, his pulse still thundering in his ears, he felt his resentment slip. No matter what she'd done in the past, he had to hand it to her now. He'd never seen anyone try so hard.

She wasn't in condition for this trek, wasn't even equipped with good boots. She had blisters on her feet, scrapes on her legs, and she could barely stand on that ankle. And even from this distance he could see her exhaustion.

Yet she hadn't complained even once. Throughout this ordeal she had pulled her weight, determined to keep herself going. She even looked out for the dog.

And it was hard to hold on to his bitterness when she was so damned nice. It would be easier if she whined or complained, even cried. But instead, she was a great companion. She always had been. Easygoing, good-humored, sexy as hell.

The kind of woman he wanted to come home to for the rest of his life.

He shoved that thought away, unwilling to entertain

that dangerous yearning. Because no matter how much he wished things were different, he couldn't alter the past.

Panting noisily, she closed the distance between them. Then she stopped, propped her hands on her knees, and gasped for breath. Her cheeks were bright, and her dark hair tangled over her shoulders. Dirt smudged her delicate chin.

But despite her exhaustion, determination gleamed in her eyes, and he couldn't help but feel impressed. She was a hell of a fighter.

"Are you okay?" he asked.

"I'm…fine."

"Want some water?"

Still wheezing, she shook her head, sending dark curls wisping around her flushed face. "No, I'm…all right."

He doubted that, but they couldn't afford to rest yet. They were still miles away from that clearing. Worse yet, sheltered in this valley between the mountains, he couldn't tell where the fire was heading.

And that made him damned nervous.

"Hold on." He dropped his PG bag to the ground and pulled his radio from the outside pocket. Ignoring the sharp pain lancing his shoulder, he straightened and keyed the mike.

Nothing happened.

He blinked, checked the switch, and tried again. Still nothing. Dread slinked through his gut. Hell, this was all they needed.

"What's wrong?" Jordan asked, her voice high.

"Looks like the batteries died." His jaw rigid, he

jammed the radio back in his bag and pulled out his compass.

Jordan raised her hand to her throat.

"It doesn't matter," he said. He kept his voice even so she wouldn't worry. "They already know where to meet us."

"But how are we doing on time?"

"Great." As long as they flew the rest of the way. He checked the compass, relieved that they hadn't veered off course, then shoved it into his pocket.

"Look," he continued calmly. "There's a lookout ridge just after we get out of this valley. It's probably another hundred yards. If you think you can make it that far, we'll wait and take a rest then."

"I told you, I'm fine."

"Good." He swung the bag back over his shoulder and, once he was sure she was ready, headed off at a steady pace. He'd spotted the ridge earlier that morning, back on the opposite peak. He hoped they could survey the fire from there, especially now that they'd lost radio contact.

Because he sure as hell didn't want to walk into a trap.

And these were perfect blowup conditions. The steep slopes and high winds would increase the speed of the fire. And if that blaze switched paths, tunneling through the valley and igniting below them, they could never escape.

His throat clenched tight, and a cold chill snaked up his spine. He'd seen the videos, completed the training. Knew all about Mann Gulch and Storm King Mountain, when smokejumpers in conditions just like these had found themselves entrapped. They'd streamed up the mountain, dazed and panicked, trying desperately to outrun the flames, sprinting frantically for their lives. A race they were destined to lose.

And the same thing could happen to them here.

His nerves tighter than a parachute's shroud lines, he rammed his worries to the back of his mind, where they wouldn't distract him from the task at hand. Instead, he focused on slugging up the steep slope toward the ridge so he could find the best way to safety.

But his body protested with every step. His skull banged beneath his hard hat. The dull ache pulsing his shoulder now racked him with piercing pain. And if he felt this lousy, he couldn't imagine how Jordan kept up.

He glanced back, and regret surged through his chest. He wished he could help her more. If his damn shoulder would cooperate, he'd carry her over the mountain. She didn't weigh much more than a loaded pack.

Too bad she didn't have crutches. He frowned, wondering why that hadn't occurred to him before. This deep in the forest, he could easily find a walking stick.

He kept an eye out for likely branches as he continued hiking. He had plenty to choose from. It had been decades since a fire had burned through, leaving the area choked with deadfall and brush. Which made the forest ripe for a massive fire, especially in these drought conditions. One good spark, either from lightning or a drifting ember, would ignite the entire peak.

Which didn't help their chances of escape.

He finally spotted a downed branch that looked the right width. He swung the bags off his shoulder, used his foot as leverage to break off the smaller side shoots, then hefted it in his hand. "This should work."

"For what?"

"A walking stick." He turned and handed it back. "Maybe you can take some weight off that ankle."

"Oh." A slow smile spread over her face, lighting her eyes to a golden brown. "I should have thought of that myself. Thank you."

Their eyes held, and for a moment, his world careened to a halt. His breath backed up in his chest, and every nerve seemed to stretch.

He forced himself to inhale. It was only a stick, for God's sake. He hadn't done anything special. But that smile of hers had the most amazing effect on him, making him feel as if he'd conquered the world.

Still feeling off balance, he picked up the bags and resumed hiking. She'd always had that effect on him. She'd made him feel whole, valued, as if he were really worthwhile.

Just like smokejumping did. It was the only place he'd found validation, where he could do everything right.

And he'd do this right, too. He'd get them safely off this mountain.

Focusing back on that goal, he angled steadily across the steep slope, skirting jagged stobs and bushes. A small animal dove into a stand of huckleberry as he passed, rustling through the dense brush and shaking the leaves. Yards later, the trees thinned out, and he turned again to check her progress.

"This is great," she told him as she hobbled up. "Just what I—"

The dog abruptly stopped. The leash went taut and she stumbled, staggering to regain her balance. She thrust out the stick to break her fall just as Cade leaped back and grabbed her.

"Thanks." Wincing, she steadied herself against him.

The contact jolted along his nerves, and he tightened his grip on her waist. She felt soft and warm, and way too good in his arms.

"Are you all right?" he murmured.

"I'm fine. He just caught me by surprise." Her lips curved into a grimace. "But I'm glad I had the stick. I would have fallen without it."

"Yeah." His gaze met hers. The air seemed suddenly thick, and he could barely pull it into his lungs.

She stepped away, her cheeks flushed, and he reluctantly released her. Then she looked at the dog, tugged on the leash, and huffed. "What's wrong? What are you doing, silly? Come on."

She pulled again, but the dog sat down and lifted his nose.

She planted her hands on her hips. "He won't budge. I guess he must be tired."

"Maybe." He watched the dog scent the air. And maybe he smelled something they didn't.

Unease chilled his gut. Even with his better nose, that dog shouldn't smell the smoke yet. Unless the fire had jumped the river and pushed the front over that mountain. Or the wind had shifted early and the fire was heading their way.

Which meant they had to get out of here fast.

"Come on," he said to the dog, his tone brusque. "Let's go."

With a little whine, Dusty rose and trotted forward.

"Well, that's interesting," Jordan said. "He wouldn't listen to me."

Cade grunted, more concerned about the fire than the dog's behavior. He moved quickly back into the lead, staying alert for signs of the blaze. He heard an air tanker rumble in the distance. Dropping more mud, he hoped.

Then the pine branches creaked overhead, and a warm breeze fanned his face. Relieved, he glanced up at the swaying treetops. That wind meant they'd made it out of the valley. They couldn't be far from the ridge.

But then another gust blew past, trailing the faint smell of smoke, and his pulse slammed to a halt. The dog was right. That fire was closer than he'd expected.

"Cade?" Jordan said, her voice pitched high. "Do you smell that?"

"We're doing fine," he called back. "It's just drifting smoke."

Which shouldn't be anywhere near them right now. It was still too damned early. That wind should blow north until tonight.

He balled his good hand into a fist, wishing to God he could see that fire. He hated hiking through this forest blind.

Because if he'd learned anything in his years of smokejumping, it was to trust his instincts. And right now, every nerve in his body urged him to get to that clearing fast.

But Jordan couldn't move any quicker. Even hiking this slowly, the woman had clearly reached her limit.

Hoping to shorten the route, he slanted directly up the steep slope. But then her pace fell off even further, forcing him to drop back. Her breathing sawed in the mountain air.

"I'm sorry," she wheezed when she'd caught up. "I know I'm holding you back."

"You're doing great."

"Hardly." She shot him a skeptical look. "I can't believe you do this for a living. You're in incredible shape."

"You get used to it. And it's not always so rough." He decided it wouldn't hurt to keep talking. It might take her mind off her pain and help her get to the ridge.

And keep him from worrying about that fire.

"The first couple days on a fire can be hard," he said as they continued walking. "The goal is to contain it fast, before it spreads. So that first night nobody sleeps. We automatically push through until morning."

"That must be tough."

"Yeah, but everyone expects it. And strong coffee helps."

Despite her fatigue, she shot him a smile, a genuine one that played along the edges of her mouth and lit up her eyes. He grinned back. She'd always shuddered at the sludge he'd brewed.

"After that, it depends on the fire and how long we stay out there. The fire lies down at night when the wind dies, so that gives us a few hours to rest."

"That's still not much."

"You get used to it." And after a while, it became a way of life. Crawling into his hootch near dawn, filthy and exhausted, his arm muscles trembling, his lungs burning from choking back smoke.

Lying under the moaning pine trees, his body spent,

too tired even to doze. Listening to the fire crackling around him and the hypnotic wail of the wind.

And with that exhaustion, in those moments of weakness, the loneliness came creeping back, the vulnerability. The thoughts of Jordan.

When he was too damned tired to fight off the truth anymore. When his anger slipped, and he yielded to that soul-wrenching need. That longing for what he could never have.

The wish that she'd loved him enough to wait.

And despite it all, night after night, he found himself aching for her, wanting her, wondering what he could have done to make her stay.

Another gust of smoke drifted by, and he shook himself back to the present. He glanced at her, and saw she was now limping badly. Her face was furrowed in concentration, and lines of pain etched her brow. That ankle had to hurt like hell, but she still persevered.

And suddenly, he knew that the next time he lay alone in the darkness, he'd picture her like this. He'd remember her spirit, her strength, her determination.

But willpower alone wouldn't get her up this mountain. He had to keep her mind off the pain. "Once we get the fire contained, the work gets easier," he said.

"How? You still have to pack out your stuff."

"Yeah, but that's easier than fighting the fire."

"Right." Her tone told him she wasn't fooled.

"And we don't always pack it out. Sometimes, if we've got a lot of equipment, they do a long-line gear retrieval. That's when a helicopter comes by and picks it up with a net.

"And if the season's really busy, they even fly us out. So we can get back on the jump list and be ready for another fire."

"But not normally."

"No, usually once the fire's out, we pack up our gear and hike to the nearest road. We leave a couple of people behind to cold-trail the fire." A fire could look as though it was out, but still smolder for weeks. So they had to go through on their hands and knees, digging out stumps, making sure it was out.

She wiped her forehead on her sleeve and wheezed in a breath. "I remember. You always stayed behind to do that."

"Choice from the top, boned from the bottom."

"Meaning?"

"That I didn't have a choice. I had to stay. You're not always first on the list."

She blinked. "Oh, I thought…"

"What? That I didn't want to come home?"

"Well, I…"

A stark stab of bitterness jolted his chest. Hell. "How could you think that?" Didn't she know him at all?

"I'm sorry, I—" She cringed. "Oh, God. I assumed you were like my father, living for your job. I…I should have asked."

"Yeah."

And maybe he should have explained.

That thought caught him off guard, and he frowned. He'd figured she understood his world and what he did. But what if she really hadn't?

He thought about what she'd said before. That they

hadn't talked much when they were married. She was right. They hadn't explained themselves. He hadn't thought it mattered.

But apparently, he'd been wrong. And suddenly, he needed to redeem himself, to make her understand. Even after all this time.

He stopped. Her dark eyes rose to meet his. "Look, Jordan." He rubbed the nape of his neck. "I like my job. I always have. But just so you know, I didn't want to leave you back then. I wasn't trying to get away."

"I know." Her dark gaze softened. And suddenly, he saw the vulnerability in those beautiful eyes, the doubt.

And he felt like the worst kind of fool. She hadn't understood. Not enough. And that explained so much. Her loneliness. The tears. The fights.

Feeling guilty, he reached out and tucked a wisp of hair behind her ear. "I felt lonely, too," he admitted, his voice gruff. "I thought about you all the time. And I always wanted to come home to you."

"Cade, I..." Her voice trembled. Her dark eyes stayed on his. "Thank you," she whispered. "I guess I needed to hear that."

"Yeah." And suddenly, deep in his gut, the tension eased. And the long years of bitterness began to unfurl.

He should have told her back then. It might have made a difference. Or maybe not. He would never know.

And it didn't change anything now. She still didn't want a smokejumper, and he wouldn't give up his job. But at least they'd settled something, put some closure on the past. And maybe regained some trust.

His throat felt thick, his head dizzy. Then a whiff of

smoke drifted past on the breeze and he pulled his gaze away. “We need to keep moving.”

“I know. Come on, Dusty,” she cooed to the dog, her voice lilting. Her gaze met his again as they started hiking. “I’m sorry I’m so slow. I know I’m holding you up.”

“You’re doing fine, really.”

“You’d be farther ahead without me.”

He couldn’t deny that. “I don’t mind the company, though.” In fact, there was no one he’d rather be with.

It was true, he realized with a start. He wanted to spend time with this woman. Somewhere in their hike across the mountains, he’d lost the urge to get away.

Which meant his resistance to her was crumbling.

And that put him in more danger than any fire.

Chapter 12

So he'd let himself become vulnerable to Jordan.

Cade battled through the thick mountain brush, that thought mired in his mind. Despite his defenses, she'd managed to suck him back in, luring him with her seductive warmth, that sense of caring. Tempting him with that relentless heat that flared whenever she was in sight.

He locked his jaw against the need to believe her. So what if she seemed sincere? He'd trusted her before, and she'd run off. Was she any more reliable now? Or was she only setting him up for another fall?

Did it matter? They weren't married anymore. They wouldn't need to see each other once they got off this mountain.

He blinked away the sweat stinging his eyes, and sighed. Yeah, it mattered. For some damn reason he couldn't let go of that woman or purge her from his heart. She'd worked herself so deeply into his soul that nothing could pry her loose.

But he couldn't dwell on that now, couldn't let himself get distracted, not with the fire this close. He'd wade through his relationship with Jordan when they were safe.

And hope to God that by then, he could bash some sense into his brain.

He checked his watch, and the unease that had haunted him all day twisted his nerves. Even at their slow pace, they should be close to that spur ridge by now. They'd been hiking for hours.

And he felt every second of it. A jackhammer shrilled in his skull. Hunger gnawed deep in his gut. His shoulder burned so badly that nausea swelled up his throat.

And if he felt this weak, he couldn't imagine how Jordan kept moving. That ankle had to be killing her by now. And they still had miles to go, hours battling through steep, brushy terrain with that damn fire heating their steps.

He just hoped to God that she could make it.

He forged a path around a thick stand of huckleberry bushes and a gust of smoke-tinged wind brushed his face. He looked up, his chest heaving, and glimpsed a slice of sky through the trees. So they'd finally reached the ridge. The tension squeezing his gut slacked. Maybe now he could get a visual on that fire and figure out the fastest way to the top.

Hurrying now, he burst through the last few pine trees onto a rocky ledge. One glance, and his hopes tanked. He couldn't see anything that would help him.

Douglas fir towered up both sides of the ridge and obscured his view of the clearing. Straight ahead, a smoke bank piled over the valley, shrouding it in gray.

He turned to warn Jordan as she limped out of the trees behind him. "You'd better stay back. There isn't much room out here." Beyond him, the rock ledge sheered off abruptly, plunging thirty feet to the trees below.

"All right. Come on, Dusty." The dog lunged and bucked, spooked by the strong smell of smoke. Hauling hard on the leash, Jordan dragged him back to the trees.

Cade pulled his own attention back to the mountain. He searched the pines on the uphill flank, but they shielded the clearing from view. Across the ridge on the eastern slope, the trees descended to the thick haze below. Between the peaks, the dense smoke pooled around the mountain, its edges fringed with dark charcoal. Further out, it boiled up white and fluffy, like innocent cumulus clouds.

But that fire was anything but harmless. Bright orange flames flicked through the heavy smoke, like the menacing breaths of a dragon. And beneath that thick cover, the blaze moved steadily forward, shaking the valley with an ominous roar.

And he couldn't tell where it was heading. He dragged his hand over his eyes, rubbing against the sting of burning pine, and wished to hell that his radio worked. He urgently needed an update.

Acknowledging the futility of that wish, he headed back to Jordan. She stared at the smoky valley, her dark eyes huge in her pale face, her smooth jaw slack with fear.

His gut fisted in recognition. He'd seen that same

look on the faces of rookies making their first jump from the plane.

And sometimes, a rookie was so damned scared that he froze in the door, unable to make himself leap. That ended his days as a smokejumper.

But unlike the rookies, they didn't have a backup plan out here. A jump ship wouldn't whisk them back to the base if Jordan balked. They had to get themselves to that clearing.

Which meant he needed to calm her down fast. He strode the final distance to the tree line. "Let's take a break and have some water," he said, his tone even. "I could use a rest, and you need to get your weight off that ankle."

Her eyes still wide, she yanked her gaze from the smoke. "But do we have time?"

"A few minutes, anyways." They couldn't stay long, but a brief rest might settle her nerves.

A line furrowed her forehead, but she nodded. "All right. I still have that orange if you want it."

"Sure, as long as you can peel it. I don't think I'd do too well with my teeth."

As he'd hoped, she managed a thin smile, then settled beside him in the parched grass.

"How does the fire look?" she asked, her voice trembling.

"According to the forecast, it should stay on the other ridge, at least until tonight." But anything could happen. And if all hell broke loose, he needed her to keep a cool head.

She looped the makeshift leash around her leg and

under her hip to secure it. The dog paced nervously, then abruptly dropped to her side.

"How's your ankle?" he asked.

"Fine." Her lips tightened, and the skin around her eyes pinched. "How's your shoulder?"

He slanted his head. "About as fine as your ankle." He handed her his canteen.

Their gazes caught, and she smiled, an amazingly brave smile that sparked laughter deep in her eyes.

And suddenly, the tension around them eased, and that connection seeped into his blood, that friendship that felt as comfortable as his worn-in smokejumper boots.

Maybe that was why they hadn't talked much when they'd been married. Because just being together felt so damned good.

A blush rose along her cheeks, and she looked away. Wisps of dark, silky hair curled around her chin and tumbled over her shoulders as she raised the canteen to her mouth.

And he wondered how many hours he'd spent just like this, watching her, entranced by her beauty and grace. Absorbed by every detail about her, from the lush, dark lashes fringing her molten eyes to the sensual way that she moved.

She finished drinking, then pulled the dog's bowl from her bag with her gentle hands, filled it and set it down. Still shaking, the dog rose and lapped the water.

She took another gulp from the canteen and gave it back. "Thanks." Her soft lips curved again, and the movement made his body hum. Then she pulled the orange from the bag and peeled it.

He inhaled, forcing air to his mesmerized brain, and eased it back out. Shc hypnotized him, all right, emptying his head so he couldn't think straight. But for both their sakes, this wasn't the time to lose focus.

He forced his gaze to the burning valley. The fire appeared to be heading north, with the main thrust on the opposite peak. But the haphazard wind gusts could still spark spot fires in any direction. And he wouldn't see them beneath the thick haze of smoke.

"I hope you didn't leave anything important in that Jeep," he said.

She shot him a startled look. "You think the fire got it?"

"Maybe. It's hard to say with the wind shifting back and forth. But I'd guess it jumped the river and is making a hard run over the mountain."

A small line creased her forehead and she frowned out at the swirling smoke. After a moment, she brought her gaze back to his. "That means our cabin's gone, too."

"Yeah." Their gazes held.

And without warning, the air between them hung still, held immobile by the weight of the past. And memories piled up, images of when they'd been happy. Of Jordan smiling, her brown eyes gleaming with laughter. Of Jordan naked, her beautiful face taut with desire. His rapture at being with the one person on earth who met his needs.

The pine trees moaned overhead, and a stark emptiness seeped through his gut, a feeling of loss. Not for the cabin. Anyone could rebuild that. And new pine trees would eventually replace the burned ones, filling in the black.

No, the loss struck deeper, sharper, as if, with the cabin, a time of his life had vanished. And that seemed more final than the divorce.

He watched a series of similar emotions flicker across her face—pain and loss, regret. And suddenly, he saw beyond his bitterness to the truth in her dark eyes. "So you did care."

"Yes." Her whisper sent heat to his chest. "Of course I cared. God, I loved you so much."

But then why the hell had she left?

"Cade, I—" She lifted her hand, then closed her mouth and shook her head.

She didn't continue, and he sucked in a breath. The acrid smoke burned his lungs and pulled him back to the present. The fire. Their survival. That last steep stretch to the clearing.

This wasn't the time to ask questions and rehash their past. He would figure all that out later, after that chopper airlifted them out.

When he had time to demand some answers.

She gave him a section of orange and cleared her throat. "So, it's a good thing we switched directions."

"Yeah."

"But is it... Can the fire—"

"I doubt it." He hated to lie, but she didn't need him fueling her fears. "But I don't really know," he added, compelled to be honest. "The way this wind's shifting, anything can happen."

He swallowed the orange, took a deep slug of water and handed her back the canteen. Thinking hard now, he strode to the ledge to plot their course. To get to the clearing, they had to continue climbing up the south face of the mountain. The trek would be steep and slow, especially with Jordan's sore ankle.

What bothered him was that he couldn't see around the spur ridge. With the tall trees blocking his view, he couldn't see where they needed to go. And if a finger of flame crept off the front and ignited this side…

Dread cramped his gut, and he tamped down the slither of fear. If only he could crank up that radio. He needed an update from dispatch, or for one of those tanker pilots to relay the view from the sky.

But his batteries were dead, and he couldn't call, which meant they had to keep hiking. They didn't have a choice. It was their only way off this mountain.

But he'd damn well better find an escape route in case that fire blew up. And with all the unburned fuel in this forest, he didn't know how he'd manage that. They needed a burned-out section, another rock slide, something that fire would skirt around. And he hadn't seen anything like that for miles.

He strode back to Jordan. She scrambled to her feet, her eyes locked on his. "Are you ready?" she asked, her voice quivering.

"Yeah." He lifted their bags while she wrapped the leash around her fist and picked up her stick.

His gaze met hers again when she straightened. "We're going to keep angling up the mountain. We'll zigzag to make it easier, but it's probably going to be steep. We need to get around to the south side where that clearing is."

"I understand."

Worry lurked in her dark chestnut eyes, along with fear. And he knew that she really did understand. This was it. They might not have another chance to talk. If that fire blasted up this mountain, they'd be running for their lives.

"Cade," she whispered. Her beautiful eyes tugged at his heart.

"Yeah." Unable to resist, he reached out and ran his thumb over her soft cheek. The smooth skin blazed through his nerves, swamping him with sensations, like a gentle voice calling him home.

Her thick, dark lashes shadowed her creamy cheeks as her gaze fell to his mouth. A shiver rose on his skin, and then the world seemed to stop, as if binding them together one last time.

And suddenly, he needed to kiss her, to touch her. To feel that soothing warmth deep in his soul.

As if reading his mind, she inched closer. He angled his head as she closed her eyes, and he slid his lips over hers. He tasted her sultry heat, her delicate sweetness, and felt her gentle breath mingle with his, just as he had a thousand times before and wanted to again.

She trembled against him and her quiet sigh called to his heart. To the part in him that yearned for her comfort, her love.

He cupped her smooth jaw with his good hand and tilted her head up to his. Then he deepened the kiss, moving past comfort into need. Surrendering to the male instincts that pulsed in his blood.

She lifted her hand to his neck, and her gentleness made his heart swell. God, he'd missed her. He'd burned for her, ached for her, during all those lonely nights.

She was sweet and warm, and the sexiest woman he'd ever known. One look, one touch, and urgency ripped through his veins.

She'd clawed so deep into his heart that even after all these years, he couldn't let her go.

But he had to. They had to get moving. Reluctantly, he broke the kiss, then watched as her eyes inched open and her smoldering gaze lifted to his. Desire blurred her eyes, and something more. His heart jerked in recognition.

"Cade," she said, her voice wobbling. She swallowed and her throat muscles moved. "I…I'm glad you're here."

"Yeah." So was he. And he'd figure that out later.

"And I need to tell you, about when I left. I should have told you before, but I—"

"Hey." He smoothed a strand of hair from her cheek. "We'll talk about it later, okay? After we get on that chopper."

"But…" Her luminous eyes searched his. "We might not… What if we don't—"

"We'll make it," he said. He kept his gaze steady on hers. "I promise."

Her forehead creased, and her eyes clouded. She opened her mouth, as if she intended to argue, but then she closed it again. "All right. But you need to know. No matter what you think, I never meant to hurt you."

Her eyes pulled at him, urging him to trust her, and he felt his final resistance slip. His lungs swelled tight. His breath jammed up. And God help him, but he believed her. No matter what she'd done in the past, he knew she was telling the truth.

The dog darted between their legs just then, and she

looked down, breaking the spell. Cade sucked in the smoky air and stepped back. "Are you ready?"

"Yes." She managed a tremulous smile, and his heart puffed up. And for the first time, he let himself hope. For what, he didn't know. But suddenly, he had more reasons than just the fire to hurry to that clearing.

Please don't stop, Jordan pleaded silently. She tugged on the leash to get the dog moving again, then scrambled up the slope behind Cade. It was bad enough that she was slowing them down with her bad ankle. If Cade discovered that the dog kept balking, he'd insist that she let him go.

Not that she blamed Dusty for wanting to rest. She'd passed exhaustion miles ago. She plodded along, dazed and dizzy, her muscles trembling, planting one blistered foot in front of the other, stumbling over rocks and branches, just praying that she would stay upright.

And her ankle! A wild moan rose in her throat. She'd managed to hide it from Cade, but the fierce pain roiled through her nerves, making her clammy and nauseous. Leaning on the stick helped her foot, but the pressure had worked her palm raw. She didn't know how she could make it to that clearing.

But she had to. Anxiety pulsed at the base of her skull, threatening to overwhelm her. She'd seen Cade's expression back at the ridge. He'd covered it with his soothing tone, but she knew his nuances well.

He doubted that they would make it.

Because she was slowing them down.

Determined to move even faster, she ignored the punishing pain, and hobbled over a rotting log. Smoke snaked through the trees like a sinister fog, heightening the tension twisting her nerves. And the blasted dog kept lunging and jerking against the leash, trying to bolt downhill.

She yanked hard on the belt to keep him going, then straightened when Cade turned back. He tilted his head and watched her, those blue eyes shrewd beneath his hard hat. "How are you holding up?"

"Great." She flashed her teeth and sucked in her breath, struggling not to limp.

Those sharp eyes narrowed. "Let me know if you need to stop."

"Right." As if they could spare the time.

"It shouldn't be far," he added. "The trees are starting to thin, which means we're near the top." He continued to study her, and she feared he'd insist that she rest. But then a breath of smoke drifted past, and he flattened his lips and turned back.

He hiked several feet ahead of her, his hard hat swiveling as he scanned the terrain. He paused occasionally to pick up some sticks, then resumed his relentless trek.

Jordan trudged along, her gaze focused on Cade's rugged frame, and the guilt she'd been battling surged back. Not just because he was working so hard, and her slow pace could cost them their lives.

No, her remorse struck deeper, darker, to those long, guilty years she'd stayed silent. To the truth that he needed to know. She should have told him about the baby back at the ridge. So what if they hadn't had time? She could have blurted it out.

But she'd been selfish. She'd wanted time to defend

herself, to explain. And, just maybe, to forge a relationship for the future.

Could they try again? He turned slightly to look up the mountain, and she studied the hard planes of his face. She loved him; she realized that now. She had never stopped.

But even if he forgave her, could she tolerate his lifestyle? Could she cope with him always being gone? Or would they only argue again?

Because she sure couldn't change who he was.

Anxiety churned through her chest, along with a deep sense of doom. Oh, God. She couldn't think about it. Not now. She hissed in a shaky breath.

Ahead of her, Cade paused and consulted his compass, then angled higher uphill. The trees were sparser now, with dry brush and grass covering the exposed slope. And it seemed quieter suddenly, more still. Or maybe the blood surging in her ears drowned the noises out.

Suddenly, Dusty stopped again. Shaken from her reflections, Jordan stumbled, staggered to regain her balance, and jerked on the leash. But this time, the dog wouldn't follow. Instead, he turned and tried to run downhill.

"Stop!" Gasping against the pain lashing her ankle, she planted her feet and leaned back. He lunged, and she widened her stance. "Stop!" she cried again. She wasn't losing him this time. She gritted her teeth and hung on.

"What's the matter?" Cade called back.

"I don't know." Dusty looked frantic now, thrashing and twisting to get free. "He's trying to go back downhill."

"Oh, hell. Stay here."

"What?" Still fighting for control of the leash, she swiveled to look at Cade. He sprinted ahead and disappeared, and a sudden fear lashed her heart. He wasn't abandoning her. Cade would never do that. She couldn't imagine him running away.

But then, where was he going? What was wrong? She turned her gaze back to the dog.

Behind her, a wind sprang up, ruffling her neck and standing her hair on edge. A sound rose from around the mountain, a muffled rumbling, like the distant sound of a train. It grew louder, closer. Every nerve in her body tensed.

And suddenly, she understood. *The fire.* Oh, God. She gaped at the wild-eyed dog, his behavior now making sense. The fire had caught them. They weren't going to reach that clearing. They were trapped!

Her knees trembled violently. Panic surged, and a loud throbbing pulsed in her head like an earthquake rocking her brain. She dithered, shuffling back and forth, her muscles stalled, not knowing which way to go. Raw fear clawed at her throat.

And then Cade came sprinting back, his legs pumping wildly, his face more intense than she'd ever seen. He skidded to a stop beside her, swung the bags to the ground and dropped to one knee.

"We have to burn an escape route," he shouted. He threw back the flap on his PG bag and yanked out some long red sticks.

The roar behind them grew louder, thundering through her skull, and the air around them started to shake. Her brain blanked, and she panted, unable to breathe. Her nerves zapped her muscles like the strings on a marionette.

"Help me light the fusees," Cade shouted again. "We have to burn off the grass."

A huge, black ball of smoke roiled through the trees and Dusty pawed to get free. The ground shuddered. Pines swayed. And a huge rush drummed through the air.

"Pull off the tabs and strike them." Cade held out the foot-long sticks.

She gawked at him, part of her brain noting his desperation. He couldn't manage with just one hand.

But she needed to run. Flee! Panic gripped her throat. Frenzied, she jerked her gaze to the slope above her. She had to climb up there and get away.

"We can't outrun it," he shouted. "It's too fast. You have to—"

Thunder shook the air, drowning out what he wanted to say. She looked at him again, her breath puffing in frantic gasps, her mind completely blank.

His mouth was moving. His eyes beseeched her. He was pleading with her, begging her, but she couldn't hear him, even from two feet away.

Then the fire burst through the trees and she screamed. It was here! Sucking and burning, boiling and streaming, billowing and swirling their way.

Oh, God. She had to run. She needed to leave, escape!

No! Her conscience stalled her. She had to stay and help Cade.

She pulled her gaze to his and saw his urgency, his need. *He needed her.* He always had.

She let out a strangled sob. And no matter what, she couldn't leave him. She'd abandoned him once before; she'd run away when her fears had swamped her, and she wouldn't do it again.

God help her, but no matter what the cost, she wouldn't quit on him this time.

Shaking wildly, fighting every instinct she had to bolt, she forced her feet not to move.

Her palms sweating, her heart quaking, she snagged the leash on her belt loop to keep the dog close, and somehow secured the buckle.

Then she lifted her gaze to Cade's. She saw emotions flash through his eyes, relief and respect, and something else. Pride. *For her.* Her heart dipped, then ballooned in her chest.

Her gaze locked on his, she reached out and grabbed a fusee.

Chapter 13

Her heart careening against her rib cage, her hands trembling harder than a leaf in a windstorm, Jordan ripped the tab off the fusee and yanked her gaze back to Cade. "What now?" she yelled.

She knew he couldn't hear her. Behind them, the fire thundered like a screeching jet plane. But he jerked his head, indicating he'd understood. Moving quickly, he set down his flarelike fusees, grabbed one of the sticks he'd collected, then jammed it into the bottom of the fusee she held.

Understanding now, she helped cram the stick tighter into the flare. The stick extended the length of the fusee, serving as a primitive handle.

Her admiration surged. No wonder Cade had collected the sticks. He'd been preparing for this moment, watching for signs that the fire would blow up, planning ways they could survive.

Gratitude slashed through her fear, along with a swell of determination. Cade had done everything for her. Now she had to do her part. She couldn't let him down.

The wind pushed smoke over their heads again. She coughed, the acrid taste scorching her lungs, and shot a frantic glance toward the crest of the hill. Thick, dark clouds mushroomed up from the fire and billowed toward them. Bright orange flames whipped high and flicked through the rolling smoke.

Her skin prickling, her heart quailing, she blocked out the horror and focused on Cade. He grabbed the tab from her hand and peeled back the paper, then struck it against the fusee. It sparked, made a hissing sound she sensed, rather than heard above the oncoming roar, and spewed out sulfury smoke.

He dropped the tab, grabbed the fusee, and held it down to the grass. The parched grass smoked, then flared, sending a vivid orange flame streaking uphill.

And suddenly, she understood. The main fire wouldn't go through an area that had already burned. Deprived of new fuel, it would have to skirt around it. So if they burned off the grass and got inside it before the flame front reached them, maybe they could survive.

But did they have enough time? Her heart rocketing, she glanced at the fire again. The front charged toward them, streaming up through the parched pines, surging and pulsing, and exploding in piercing orange flames. Her nerves quaked, and she panted in shallow breaths. Oh, God. It was so fast, so big. How on earth could they beat it?

But they had to try. Frantic now, she kicked herself into action. She snatched another fusee from Cade's pile, rammed a stick extension in it, pulled off the tab, and lit it. She spared another glance at the booming fire, shuddered, then grabbed the remaining fusees and ran after Cade.

She waved her arm to get his attention, and he motioned to his right. Jerking the leash to keep the dog moving, she rushed along and lit the baked grass. Her nerves hopping, steeling herself against the fear that threatened to freeze her, she tried to block out the horrible roar and concentrate on her job. Fanned by the wind, their small fire raced up the grassy slope, surrounding them in a sea of flames.

Beside her, the dog twisted and charged in terror, twining around her legs and blocking her path. She grabbed the leash and yanked him out of her way. She didn't dare cut him loose; he could never outrun the fire. His only chance to survive was to stay with them.

Her panic building, struggling to control the dog and set the fire, she staggered alongside Cade. The strong sulfur smell of the fusees mixed with the acrid smoke, making her want to retch. She coughed and gagged, then blinked her stinging eyes. Tears streamed down her cheeks.

The fire boomed, and the thundering behind her grew harsher. A sob wedged in her throat, and she lurched faster, desperate to pick up her pace.

Cade sprinted back just then, his eyes fierce. Moisture streaked down his gaunt cheeks, cutting a path through the grime. He pried his spent fusee off the stick with his boot, and reached for hers.

She traded with him, grabbing his empty stick in return. While he darted back to burn more grass, she lit another flare.

Suddenly, a huge swooshing noise pulsed behind her, and, terrified, she swiveled back. A wall of flames raced toward them, twisting high into shocking funnels. Flying embers flashed through the billowing smoke. The fire shot from the trees and exploded into the air.

Then firebrands rained around them, sparking more grass. Trembling wildly, unsure what to do, she wrenched her gaze back to Cade. She felt paralyzed, frantic, torn in a thousand directions. She had to move, get away from the fire, but she didn't know where to go.

Cade turned toward her and yelled something, then motioned urgently with his arm. Understanding slashed through her hysteria. He wanted her to go up.

Terrified, praying to God that they could escape, she lunged forward and followed Cade across the charred grass. But then the dog abruptly stopped, and Jordan fell to her knees. She landed hard, singeing her palms and knees on the smoldering grass, and immediately surged to her feet. She jerked hard on the leash, but Dusty refused to budge.

Panicked, she yanked on the leash again, but the dog only hunkered down. A frenzy rose inside her. They had to run. The fire was nearly here!

A blast of hot wind swirled smoke from the blackened grass and into her face. Fueled by fear and adrenaline, every nerve in her body screaming to flee, she tossed aside her fusee, hoisted the quivering dog to her hip and darted after Cade.

A thought skittered through her brain, warning her that she should feel pain in her ankle and heat from the flames, but the terror jolting her mind blocked it out. She had to run. *Run!* Her heart pumping madly, her chest heaving, she sawed in air and sprinted uphill.

Cade charged ahead of her, stooping to torch the dry grass. A hot wind blasted their backs, and their little fire picked up speed, racing up the steep slope. Her vision blurring, her chest searing, Jordan chased the bright line of flames.

Suddenly Cade tossed aside his spent fusee and turned back. Their eyes met, and for an instant, his vivid blue gaze held hers. She saw his fierce concentration, his focus on the job. Gratitude swept through her, along with the sharp urge to cry. God, this man was brave.

Then a pounding, swooshing sound rose, and Cade's eyes flicked to the fire behind them. Her nerves jerking in disjointed spasms, Jordan stopped and turned toward the noise. Before she could look, Cade grabbed her arm and yanked her back into motion.

She stumbled, trying desperately to keep her balance while lugging the dog, and somehow pulled herself upright. Then she bolted straight up the mountain with Cade, pursuing the fire they'd set. She hauled scorched air into her lungs, breathing in ragged gasps, her throat and raw chest rasping.

Heat blasted her back, and the fierce roar pounded her skull. She tripped over rocks and uneven ground, over charred and smoking stumps. She pushed herself faster, harder, urgency fueling her steps. Embers flew past, the smoke swirled thicker and her horror grew.

They weren't going to make it. They couldn't possibly get away.

But they had to. She clutched the shaking dog, frantic not to drop him. He needed her to go on!

She kept sprinting, her feet pounding, but she could feel her exhaustion mount. She focused on Cade's strong hand gripping her arm, but still the doubts slithered in. Oh, God. She'd never make it. She was far too weak.

She would fail him, just as she had in the past.

And then a strange calm overtook her, and she felt detached, distant from her body. Smoke blurred her vision, darkening the landscape and cutting out light. The world looked surreal, bathed in a hot gray haze, bizarre.

They bounded down a slight incline, then hurdled a burning log. The fire was everywhere now, roaring and hissing beside them, the heat unbearably intense.

She ran on and on. Sprinting, climbing, leaping. And she was growing confused. She was running with Cade, clutching the dog, urgency hammering her brain, but she couldn't remember where they were or why they were racing. She only knew that she couldn't stop.

Suddenly, Cade jerked her hard to the right. She stumbled, nearly dropping the dog, and staggered to a stop. Cade pulled her toward him, and she lurched closer, staring blankly at a mound of boulders.

The air trembled, blurring her vision, and the ground beneath her rumbled and shook. She swiveled back and cringed at the fire raging toward them. Flames twisted and arced through the trees, whirling like gaseous tornadoes. A ball of flame launched itself into the air.

Cade yanked her around and pushed her toward the boulder. She saw a slit between the rocks, barely enough to squeeze through, and understanding flashed. Holding the dog close, she wriggled through the crack into a dim, musty space. Cade immediately crammed himself in behind her.

They were in a small cave, maybe a dozen feet deep and wide and barely high enough to stand in. The packed-dirt floor was littered with stones.

"We need to block the opening," Cade said, dropping the bags.

Jordan set down the dog, then tripped when he slammed against her. Hysteria plucked at her nerves. She couldn't help Cade if she kept stumbling over the leash. And Cade needed her help to survive.

Which meant she had to let Dusty go.

Her hands trembling, she unhooked the leash from her belt, then wedged it beneath a large rock. The dog immediately tried to pull free.

"Stay," she said sharply and stepped away. She could only pray the leash held. She didn't have time to hold him, and she couldn't help him if he darted outside.

Her throat thick with dread and panic, she set to work, frantically lugging rocks over to block the entrance. She dashed back and forth, piling the stones quickly, haphazardly, rushing to stop the smoke creeping through the cracks. Outside, the deadly roars and thundering grew.

Behind her, Cade pulled something from his PG bag. Silver flashed in the fading light as he shook it out.

His fire shelter. The last line of defense. The final chance to survive.

He held out the metallic fabric. "Here. Put this between the rocks."

"No." She backed off. He needed that tent. He could survive inside it without her. And she'd hindered him enough.

"Jordan—"

"It's yours. You use it."

"The hell I will." His voice bristled with outrage. "Either stuff it between those rocks or I'll flatten it over you."

He'd do it. She could see the obstinate will in his eyes, that single-minded resolve, and knew it was futile to argue. Unless she agreed to share the shelter, he'd sacrifice his own life protecting hers.

And she refused to let him do that.

Resigned, she grabbed the lightweight fabric and smoothed it over the rocks. Her heart beat erratically as she scooped up loose stones and stuffed them in the cracks to secure the edges. The light dimmed as she blocked up as many spaces as she could. Cade added several heavier stones so the shelter wouldn't blow off.

After a moment, he stopped her. "That's good enough. We need to get back."

She blinked in the shadowy darkness. Light still filtered through some gaps in the rocks, but she knew they'd run out of time. Outside, the deafening noise mounted, screaming and screeching like colliding trains. Shaking, so scared she thought she might vomit, she covered her ears and cringed.

Cade grabbed her arm and pulled her toward the back of the cave. "Wait," she cried. "The dog." She stooped down to jerk the leash loose, and dragged him to the far wall.

Cade urged her down to the ground, then positioned himself beside her, wedging her between him and the musty dirt wall. She hauled Dusty into her lap and held him close. Quivering madly, shuddering with terror, she curled herself into a ball.

She couldn't breathe, couldn't think as the heat mounted and a throbbing blast pulsed outside. She closed her eyes, and Cade pulled her head to his chest, covering her with his body.

This was it. The moment of truth.

She could only thank God Cade was with her, and pray that they would survive.

Chapter 14

Cade sheltered Jordan with his body as the firestorm raged around them. Heat scorched his back. His pulse rocketed through his veins. The hairs on his nape stood erect and tensed in the rising storm.

The air around them quivered, and a bone rattling screech shook the cave. The earth trembled, the skies shrieked as the molten gasses collided. Vibrations blurred the hot air.

His lungs seized up and his heart stalled. Sweat popped from his pores, and he gagged down his acrid fear. This was it, the moment when they'd see if the shelter held, if they'd burned enough grass to protect the cave.

To find out if they would survive.

Time hung still. An eternity pulsed in a second. He

clutched Jordan and shut his eyes, every nerve focused on the explosions blasting the cave.

And then miraculously, incredibly, the deadly noise shifted away.

He slumped in acute relief, then tipped back his head and exhaled. His heart battered against his chest, and his muscles began to twitch.

And for the first time, he let the reality sink in of just how close that had been. They'd nearly died.

He'd seen the training videos, attended classes on fire entrapments, but nothing had prepared him for the reality of it happening to him. The absolute panic, the disbelief, the horror when the fire blew close. And that gut-shaking terror when he'd realized they might not survive.

If it hadn't been for the dog… He loosened his death grip on Jordan and glanced down at the quivering fur on her lap. If that mutt hadn't balked, hadn't warned them that the fire was near…

He swallowed the thick wedge blocking his throat, unwilling to finish the thought. But the truth remained. That dog had given them the valuable seconds they'd needed to survive.

And they had survived. His hand still twined in Jordan's hair, he gently stroked her scalp to soothe her and pressed her head to his chest. Trembles wracked her body, and she shuddered with anxiety and fear.

"Shh…." he murmured. He cleared his throat, fighting to get words past the lump. "We're safe now. The fire's gone."

"Oh, God," she said, her voice muffled against his

shirt. Still shaking, she pulled back, and her fathomless gaze met his. Her eyes glistened in the cave's dim light. The remnants of tears streaked her cheeks, cutting paths through the ashes and grime.

But he'd never seen a more beautiful woman.

A fierce swell of emotion surged up, relief mixed with something more, that feeling he'd been fighting for days.

Love. He loved Jordan. He always had.

It was true. He'd stopped denying it the moment she'd reached for that fusee. He'd seen her horror and panic, the primitive urge to escape. But despite her terror, she'd stayed.

A thick wad of emotion choked his lungs, and he tightened his grip on her head. He could only imagine the courage, the incredible leap of faith that had taken. She wasn't a trained firefighter, didn't know wildfire behavior or the futility of running. Yet she'd ignored her instincts and trusted him.

And in that moment, he'd stopped trying to fool himself and admitted how much he loved her—this brave, gutsy woman who'd once been his.

He caressed the silky strands of her hair, ran his gaze over the smooth curve of her cheek and the feminine line of her jaw.

Her wide, dark eyes searched his, as if she couldn't grasp that they were safe. Shudders still shook her body, discharging the adrenaline and fear, the need to run, the primal instinct to flee. And he continued to stroke her head, her neck, knowing she needed the warmth, the human contact.

So did he.

"You did great out there," he said, his voice raw from emotion and smoke.

"Is it… Are you sure it's gone?" Her voice hitched on a little sob.

"Yeah, it's gone. Listen."

Her gaze flew to the entrance to the cave, which they'd been damned lucky to find. In the distance, the dull roar slid away, replaced by muffled pops. Still trembling, she gnawed her bottom lip.

Seconds later, her gaze swiveled back to his. "It won't come back? It—"

"No, it's done." He squeezed her neck to reassure her. "There'll be a few stumps burning, even some flare-ups, but as hot as that fire was, I doubt there's much left to burn."

She jerked her head, and a tremor jolted her body. Her lips quivered, and she sucked in a tremulous breath.

He saw the awareness in her eyes of just how close they'd come to dying. The stark realization that they could have burned, that the charred remains of their bodies could be out there right now, writhing and smoldering in the ashes.

"Oh, God, Cade."

"Yeah." He smoothed the knot tensing her neck and stroked the smooth skin of her nape. Then he shifted his hand to her rigid shoulders.

The dog crept off Jordan's lap, and she lunged for the leash.

"Don't worry. He can't go anywhere."

"You're right." She dropped the leash and sat back, then eased out an uneven breath. Her lips strained into a smile. "I'm just so nervous, I—"

"Hey, it's normal. Just give yourself time to come down."

Urging her back, he threaded his hand through her hair, and continued soothing her neck, giving her time to absorb the outcome, that they were safe. She leaned into him, and as the minutes passed, her breathing slowed and deepened. Her shivering gradually calmed.

And his awareness shifted to the pain ramming his shoulder, the persistent hammering in his skull. The hard dirt floor beneath him. The smoke permeating the air, mingling with the dank smell of the cave.

And Jordan's soft body pressed against his, beautiful and feminine and arousing.

Desire flashed through his veins, and his hand instinctively tightened. Battling the reaction, he tipped back his head and sucked in a breath.

He loved her; he couldn't deny it anymore. And everything about her appealed to him—the way she looked, the way she moved, the tender way she cared for the dog. Her hard work, her amazing courage. The woman had seeped into his brain and conquered his heart.

But he still couldn't forget reality, couldn't let his emotions override common sense. And the harsh fact was that she was wrong for him. No matter how much he loved her, she needed what he couldn't give her, a man who always stayed home.

And he could never be that man, not without destroying his soul.

And yet she felt perfect in his arms, and in his life. She shifted then, and their thighs touched. Her soft, full breasts pressed against his chest. The silk of her hair tickled his mouth.

She lifted her head and her eyes met his, her face just inches away. Her pupils dilated in the dusky light. Her pink tongue moistened her lips. She hitched in a ragged breath.

His hormones jerked in recognition. She wanted him. His answer rolled hard through his veins.

"Cade," she whispered.

"It's just the adrenaline," he ground out. "The near-death experie—"

"No." She raised her hand to his mouth. Her fingers clamped his lips, silencing him. The feel of that soft skin staggered his senses, and need coiled tight in his gut.

He leaned back and grabbed her wrist to push her away, but she inched forward, her dark eyes simmering on his. His lungs stalled, and he felt snared by that luminous gaze, lured into her erotic web.

And in that instant, he knew he was doomed. He needed to touch her, to taste the seductive heat of her skin. To feel her satiny body shudder under his.

His gaze locked with hers. Deliberately, he turned her hand and brushed his lips across her palm. He raked the delicate skin, skirting the scrapes, then soothed the spot with his tongue. She gasped, and the need in her eyes flared. His thumb skimmed her wrist, and he felt the erratic lurch of her pulse.

Her eyes softened into liquid darkness, and then her lids fluttered closed. Her full lips parted, and her breathing rasped faster, more shallow.

He dropped her wrist and caught her chin, then

slanted his mouth over hers. He forgot the pain wrenching his shoulder, the filth and sweat, the fire beyond the dank cave. His world narrowed to the velvet of her lips, the lush, hot silk of her mouth, and he pulled her hard against him.

She parted her lips and kissed him back. Her hands clutched his hair, and her tongue dueled with his, reeling him in deeper and harder.

Maybe it was the affirmation of life, the need to connect after nearly dying. And maybe it was love, the explosion of desire long denied.

But whatever the cause, his control slipped even more. That familiar haze fogged his brain, that insatiable heat. The heady feeling that he'd found the one woman on earth who felt perfectly right.

And was, ironically, exactly wrong.

With supreme effort, he wrenched away and pulled her head to his chest. His heart slammed against his rib cage. His breathing rasped in the smoky cave. He shut his eyes and grappled for control.

He had to stop. A kiss was one thing, but they'd strayed far too close to that dangerous edge, that line that they couldn't cross. It had always happened that way between them—too fast, too hot. Reckless need and relentless wanting.

But they couldn't give in to it again, not without regrets. Not without plummeting to that insanity that guaranteed turmoil and pain.

But she pulled free and rose to her knees. "Cade, please," she begged.

"No. It's just—"

"No, it's not." She clutched his head between her hands and her gaze pleaded with his. "It's not just the fire. It's more. It always has been. I need you. I—"

"Jordan, no." But he felt his resistance crumble.

"I need you," she whispered again. "Please."

She brushed her lips over his and kissed him again, letting him feel her desire. Working her magic with her body and tongue, fueling the torment, stoking the flames.

He felt her rush of hunger, the passion in her kiss as her hands roved his face and his jaw. Her breasts stroked his chest. Her kiss turned raw and urgent. His own needs shut down his brain.

She was good. Damned good. And hell, he was only human. She wanted him; he wanted her. Was that so wrong? And they'd almost died just now. Why shouldn't they indulge in a moment of pleasure?

With a low growl, he wrapped his arm around her waist and yanked her hard against him. Then, pulling her with him, he dropped back to the packed-dirt floor.

She landed atop him, then pulled herself upright. "Cade." Her lips were swollen, her voice breathless. "Your shoulder—"

"Forget it." It throbbed like hell, but not as much as the ache in his groin. His pulse beat hot and hard as he pulled her head down to his. Then he covered her mouth in a deep, driving kiss, fueled by years of wanting.

He felt the satin of her lips, the fever of her tongue, her soft shudders as he delved her sweet depths. He smelled smoke and desire, and woman. Jordan. *His woman.* Her scent surrounded him, invaded him, until stark need twisted his gut. Until hunger seeped so deep into his heart that it wiped out every thought—except the overwhelming desire to possess her.

Needing physical contact, needing to feel her body tight against his, he lowered his hand to her hip and pressed her back. Her soft weight settled on his groin, shorting his nerves. She rocked against him, making soft, low moans in her throat, and his heart leaped in tattered spurts. A thick, quick surge of desire jolted through him, and he groaned.

And suddenly, he needed to see her, all of her, to feel her hot, naked skin slick on his.

As if sensing his thoughts, she broke the kiss and rose to her knees. Her languid eyes rested on his, hot and dark with arousal. Her hair fell in unruly waves down her back. Her swollen lips parted in an erotic invitation to bliss.

His gaze traveled from that sultry mouth to the tantalizing curve of her breasts. To the nipples jutting beneath the tight T-shirt, beckoning for his touch.

His hand trembling, he reached up and traced the outline of her curves through the thin shirt. He stroked the tempting fullness and fondled the pebbled nipples, feeling her tremble and shudder around him.

"Oh, Cade," she whispered, her voice uneven. She reached down and lifted the hem of her shirt, then yanked it over her head. His gaze stalled on the wonder of her breasts, the stretchy scrap of lace highlighting the blinding perfection.

He tried to swallow, but his throat seemed stuffed with ashes. He wrenched his gaze to hers and saw the scalding heat, the growing hunger. The memories of those steamy, torrid nights. Of how they'd loved each other, with an honesty and passion that had left them reeling.

She flicked one strap off her shoulder and let it drop. His gaze followed the motion, just as she planned. He quirked his mouth, recognizing the ploy, but still helpless to resist it. She knew him too well. And she wielded the power to drive him wild.

It was as if this one woman had been made to match his body, his mind. As if she were his ideal counterpart, his destined mate.

And no matter how many times they'd come together, it had never been enough. He'd still felt that unending hunger and constant craving.

The other strap slid off her smooth shoulder and his pulse roared through his veins. And then she rose, lifting herself out of reach, and unhooked her bra.

The lacy scrap fell away and his gaze riveted on the swell of her breasts, the dark nipples glistening in the dim light, the utter beauty of her bare flesh.

His pulse pounded as he dragged his gaze up to hers and their eyes latched. And she mesmerized him with her need, seduced him with that slow, savage burn.

The snap on her jeans popped, and his blood leaped in expectation. The zipper rasped in the scorching silence, while his blood surged hard in his ears.

She rose to her feet and stepped aside. His gaze fell to her flat, satiny belly, to the provocative arch of her hips. Her thumbs hooked the waistband of her jeans and she inched them over her legs, down her long, lean muscles and velvet skin. His fingers curled, then flexed, yearning to skim the curving length.

His gaze fastened on the final scrap of lace glimmering in the dim light. His breathing grew labored and his heart rammed against his rib cage.

She pushed the lace down, then kicked it free. His feverish gaze swept over her, lingering on the dark thatch between her thighs and the luscious peaks of her breasts. Desire ripped through him, urgent and hot.

His gaze drove into hers. And he saw the answering heat, the clawing need. Her cheeks were flushed, her eyes sultry—with arousal and something more.

She stood before him, completely naked, exposed to his fervent gaze. Hiding nothing. Vulnerable.

The look faded from her eyes, but he felt the effects down to his soul. As if she'd reached out and twisted his heart. And instincts surged, beyond lust, to the deep-seated need to protect her, to guard her heart and keep her safe.

Thick, fierce emotions wadded his chest, and suddenly, he knew that this moment was different. That they'd experienced a connection, an honesty they'd never shared before.

But then she lowered herself to him, sliding her bare legs over his hips, and the sight of her naked skin on his fully clothed body emptied his mind. She rubbed against him, stroking the hard, rigid length of him in a movement so erotic that pleasure bolted straight to his groin.

He cupped her breast and watched her limpid eyes close. Her head tipped back and her full lips parted. Her wild hair tumbled over her back.

His body was rock hard now, his muscles rippling with impatience. "Jordan." His voice sounded dredged from the earth.

"Yes." She shifted to one side and unzipped his pants. And the feel of her gentle hands on him nearly made him weep.

Almost unable to form a coherent thought, he grasped for sanity. He forced his throat to work. "Jordan, wait. I—I don't have anything, any protection."

Her eyes met his, and he saw the flash of pain. And he remembered when they hadn't needed protection, when they'd made love skin to skin.

"It's all right," she said. "It's not the right time."

"But—"

"It's all right, Cade. I promise." And then she slid over him and took him slowly into her body. Into the hot, tight flesh, to the delirium of pleasure. And the protests died in his throat.

He gave in and surrendered to rapture. And she moved against him, scalding him with her heat, stoking the flames, creating a need so violent that it dragged a groan from his heart.

He surged upward, driving into her, and felt her unravel. Her breath came in shallow gasps, her forehead furrowed. Her eyes closed and her lips parted, and she let out a keening cry.

He hooked his arm around her neck and pulled her face down to his. And then he fused his mouth to hers, claiming her, branding her with a deep, torrid kiss with no restraints. Honest and savage and raw.

And then he gave one last thrust and exploded inside her. Waves of pleasure jolted his senses. Dire need melded with bliss. He was where he belonged, with the woman he loved.

And as the tremors slowly ebbed, and the urgency subsided back into need, he wondered again how she could have left him, how she could have tossed this amazing love away.

The whomp of an approaching helicopter crept into the silence. It grew louder, its rotors thumping as it passed over the cave. Their ride home had finally arrived. And the spurt of relief he felt was mixed with a strange reluctance.

Jordan lifted herself to her knees, looking dazed, then wobbled to her feet. Her gaze met his for an instant, guilty and grim, and then it skittered away.

And his frustration surged. What the hell did that look mean? Was she suddenly having regrets? She was the one who'd insisted.

Tired of her games, he rolled to his feet and zipped his pants. And without warning, the weight of the past ordeal pressed upon him. His body felt flayed, his stomach empty. Pain rammed his skull. His shoulder shuddered and ached.

And the futility of it all overwhelmed him, draining the last trace of pleasure from his blood. And he felt angry, damned angry. He was tired of being jerked around, sick of her damned evasions. Always wondering, never knowing. And he wanted answers now.

He turned to face her. She'd put on her jeans and bra, and had her T-shirt poised in her hand. Her gaze met his, and she paused.

His jaw hardened. His stomach clenched, and he moved deliberately closer. She stepped back. He leaned into her space, trapping her, until her dark eyes widened and her skin paled under the ashes. The scent of their love-making lingered in the air, stoking his anger into rage.

"So," he said, his voice completely flat. "Just why the hell did you leave?"

Chapter 15

Jordan felt the blood drain from her face, and she froze. She stared into Cade's furious blue eyes, her heart beating a fast, irregular rhythm against her throat. This wasn't how she'd wanted to tell him. Not with him angry. Not with the helicopter circling outside.

Not when the most tender, exquisite experience of her life still pulsed in her nerves, lovemaking so perfect that it had shattered her heart.

Hardly breathing, she dropped her gaze to the T-shirt balled in her fist. She pried her fingers loose and shook it out, feeling suddenly exposed. Needing to regain some distance, she pulled the soiled shirt over her head and smoothed it down.

And braced herself for the confrontation. Even if the

timing wasn't ideal, Cade needed to know the truth. He'd deserved to hear it ten guilty years ago.

And she couldn't put it off any longer.

Her stomach tensing, she forced her gaze up to his. A muscle in his cheek ticked, and his lean jaw tightened beneath the stubble.

She hitched in an unsteady breath. "When you left on that last trip, I…I was pregnant."

He blinked. Then his jaw slackened, and for a second he looked stunned, as if she'd said the last thing he'd ever expected.

But then his expression stilled and his eyes turned blank. His wide shoulders stiffened, and she realized he'd misunderstood.

"Cade, no." She reached out to touch his arm and he flinched back. His rejection flayed her, like a whip on her raw nerves. "I didn't…I mean, I lost the baby. I miscarried. I didn't—" Oh, God. "I *never* would have had an abortion."

A dull red stain inched up his neck, but his expression only turned colder. And she realized she was botching it badly. Everything was coming out wrong.

She twisted her hands, then rubbed her palms on her thighs, searching for a way to explain. "I found out just after you left."

"And you didn't think I needed to know?"

The flat fury in his tone made her cringe. "Of course I did. I wanted to tell you right away. I was so happy and excited, and I wanted that baby so badly. But I wanted to tell you in person, to see your face when I broke the news."

She had envisioned that romantic moment, had played it all out in her head. The music and candles. The tenderness in his sexy blue eyes. The joy.

"I thought you'd be coming back soon," she whispered.

She searched his eyes, hoping for some sign of softness, but his hard face stayed unrelenting. And a sinking feeling filled her gut. He wasn't going to make this easy—which was probably what she deserved.

"And then, when you called to tell me you'd gone to Alaska, I just…I felt abandoned, betrayed." Crushed by the anger and hurt. Dazed that the man she had trusted had left her, and that her worst fear had finally come true.

She forced air into her lungs. "I started cramping after that. And I…"

She closed her eyes, remembering the panic and fear. She'd been nineteen years old and surrounded by strangers, more alone than she'd felt in her life.

She clutched her trembling hands together, then gestured, helpless to stem the old pain. "I didn't know what to do. I drove to the hospital. They told me there wasn't anything I *could* do, that I just needed to rest. So I went back to the apartment."

She shifted her gaze to the cave's dark wall, her mind focused on the agony of the past. How she'd lain on that sagging plaid couch, scared and lonely, afraid to move, and desperately needing Cade.

"And then…I just started bleeding and it wouldn't stop." She pressed her fingers to her lips and closed her eyes until the horror passed, until the shocking visions receded. Then she fixed her gaze on Cade. “And I drove back to the hospital.”

“Alone?” A muscle twitched in his cheek.

“Yes, I… They admitted me, but I still lost the baby.” Her chest wadded up with remembered feelings, that soul-numbing pain and grief. The guilt that she’d done something wrong and had somehow been to blame.

And as she’d lain there in that hospital bed, her hopes and dreams crashing down, the harsh reality had sunk in. She wouldn’t have that cozy family. Cade wanted to smokejump more than he loved her. She was alone, abandoned, just as she’d always feared.

He worked his jaw. “And you didn’t call me.” It wasn’t a question. They both knew that she hadn’t. The base would have patched an emergency message through.

“I didn’t think…” She spread her hands. “I thought you wouldn’t want—”

“To come back when my wife was in the hospital?” He stared at her, his face etched with disbelief.

A tight ball formed in her chest. “I thought you’d rather stay on the fire.”

“Hell.” The muscles along his jaw tensed, and he curled his hand into a fist, looking angrier than she’d ever seen him. “You didn’t give me a goddamn chance.”

She couldn’t deny it. She had made assumptions, big ones. And she hadn’t let him decide. “You’re right,” she whispered. “I’m sorry.”

His eyes narrowed in disgust, and then he turned and stalked to their bags. Despair spiraled through her as he hefted them up.

“Cade,” she pleaded.

He strode to the entry without answering, and in one furious movement yanked his fire shelter loose.

Stones fell and crashed around him, and the dog bolted to the back of the cave. Sunlight slanted through the rising dust, and he kicked the loose rocks aside. Then, without looking back, he twisted out of the opening and disappeared.

A sick, heavy feeling churned through her belly, and suddenly, like the pile of stones falling, the truth tumbled in on her, sucking the air from her lungs. She'd told herself he didn't care, that he loved smokejumping more than her.

But it wasn't true. He would have come home. He would have rushed to her side if she'd called him. He never would have ignored her needs, her pain, no matter how busy he'd been. He wasn't that kind of man.

She raised her hand to her throat. Of course Cade would have come back, and he would have mourned with her, grieved with her, stayed with her, just as he'd helped her over the mountain.

A sense of foreboding slugged through her chest. Oh, God. What had she done?

Her nerves trembling, she snatched up the leash and squeezed through the crack in the rocks, pulling Dusty behind her. Once outside, she stopped and blinked in the startling brightness.

She raised her hand to shade her eyes and glanced around, stunned by the devastation. The fire had decimated the mountain, turning the once-green landscape into blackened wreckage. Smoke still simmered over the scorched earth, wafting and swirling through ashes.

Charred trees bent at odd angles, like twisted silhouettes clawing the sky. Here and there, lingering flames crackled through burnt stumps and spewed out dying embers.

She breathed in the acrid stench, coughed, and blinked again. The sunshine seemed too bright in the ruined landscape, too stark. As if it were stripping away her pretenses and exposing the truth, revealing her insecurities and fears.

Her guilt.

Her breathing ragged, she scanned the hillside for Cade. She spotted him several yards away atop a charred knoll, staring down the mountain. His back was straight, his shoulders stiff, warning off any approach.

Or maybe he was grieving for the child he'd never known.

An awful tightness wrenched her throat, and she knew that she had to reach him. "Cade," she said.

His shoulder jerked as if she'd struck him, and then he slowly turned to face her. His face was tight, his mouth flat, his eyes so distant she shivered. Anxiety climbed up her throat.

"I'm sorry," she said. "I was wrong. I shouldn't have assumed you wouldn't come back. That wasn't fair to you. And I should have told you about the baby."

For several heartbeats, he didn't speak. His gaze stayed on hers, frank and cold, as if he were weighing her words, measuring her sincerity. Her hopes plummeted even more.

Finally, he tilted his head. "You didn't want me to come back, did you?"

"What?" Shock tightened her voice. "Of course I wanted you back. How can you even think that?"

He slowly shook his head, his eyes hard. "No, you were looking for an excuse to leave."

Denials rose in her throat, along with a spurt of panic. "You're wrong. I felt abandoned without you. I hated being alone." And she'd dreaded a lifetime spent waiting.

"Then why didn't you call?"

"I—" A sliver of doubt crept through her mind. Why hadn't she called him? How had she misjudged his character so badly? Hadn't she known her husband at all?

Dread piled in as she considered the implications and fought the conclusion sickening her gut. And then suddenly, she couldn't avoid it any longer. The truth crashed into her mind.

Stricken, she sucked in her breath. "Oh, God. You're right." At least in a way. "I wanted you back, but only under my terms." To fulfill her needs, her insecurities.

But he hadn't played into that. He'd treated her like a woman, not a child. He'd expected her to cope when he was gone.

And she couldn't handle that. She'd acted out the needs of her childhood, thrusting him into a role he didn't deserve. Punishing him for the faults of her father. Ignoring the person he was.

And then when he didn't play her game, she'd seized the excuse to flee.

And in the process, she'd destroyed something special, something unique, something she'd never find again. She'd taken the gift of this man's love and tossed it away.

Their eyes stayed locked, and sick dread lurched through her gut. Her heart wrenched with remorse; her face burned with guilt and chagrin. She wanted to weep with the awful realization of how unfairly she'd acted and how badly she'd hurt this man.

She couldn't excuse what she'd done and had no way left to fix it.

The reverberations of the helicopter broke the tense silence. They grew louder, filling the air with a whomping sound. The dog jerked against the leash, and she tightened her grip to hold him.

Then a shadow crossed overhead, and the ashes swirled by her feet. The helicopter hovered just beyond the cave, then headed for the clearing.

"It's over," Cade said, his face devoid of expression. "Let's go."

Whether he meant their ordeal or their relationship didn't matter. Both were finished.

Feeling completely battered inside, she picked up the dog and followed Cade through the ashes to catch their ride.

Chapter 16

"He's gone?" Jordan gaped at the nurse sitting behind the emergency room desk. "But he can't be, not with his bad shoulder. A tree crushed him. My God, his head, his ribs, he—"

"Honey, I'm not the doctor. I don't decide what the patients can do." The nurse leaned back and crossed her arms over her flowered scrubs.

"I know, but he—" Jordan clamped down hard on her lip, knowing it was pointless to argue. This nurse couldn't control where Cade spent the night.

But she had to see him, talk to him. She twisted her bandaged hands, her sense of urgency rising. She couldn't let their trip end this way.

Even if that was what Cade intended.

He obviously didn't want to see her. He'd ignored her

on the flight to Missoula, looking more remote than when their journey had started. And once they'd landed at the hospital, he'd handed the dog over to his smokejumping friend, Trey Campbell, and let the nurses lead him away.

He hadn't looked back, hadn't asked to see her again. And now he'd left the hospital without even saying goodbye.

Or had he?

She thought back to those final moments on the mountain, to his hurt over her deception. To the bitterness in his blazing blue eyes. And she realized that he had said goodbye. She just hadn't wanted to hear it.

But she couldn't let it end like this. Panic surged and then engulfed her, like a wildfire searing her chest. She needed to find him, plead with him.

Tell him she still loved him.

But arguing with this nurse wouldn't help. She sucked in a steadying breath. "Look, I'm sorry. I just really need to see him. Could you at least tell me his address? I think he has an apartment nearby."

"Sorry, we're not allowed to give out that information."

"I'm sure he wouldn't mind. He's my ex-husband. We—"

"There's a telephone book in the lobby. You're welcome to look in that."

"But what if he's not listed? He might only have a cell phone."

"Sorry." The nurse returned her gaze to her computer screen.

Knowing it was futile to argue, Jordan curbed her

frustration and stepped back. She could head to the smokejumper base and ask, but they weren't open at night. And they might refuse to tell her, too.

"Excuse me, ma'am?"

Jordan turned. A nurse pushing a gurney paused by the desk, waiting for her to move.

"Oh, I'm sorry." Her face warming, she steadied her crutches and moved aside. She couldn't take up these people's time when others had more serious problems.

She'd been lucky on that mountain. Aside from a mildly sprained ankle and a few lost pounds, she'd survived the ordeal intact. And after giving her a tetanus booster, antibiotics and an IV to replace lost fluids, the doctor had allowed her to leave. All she needed now was a hot shower and a few days of rest to bring her body back to normal.

If she could only do the same for her heart.

The nurse wheeled the gurney past, and she caught a glimpse of the young man on it. He looked pale against the sheets, his features racked with pain.

And suddenly, her stomach flipped and her heart stalled. And she couldn't stop the memories from slamming through her, of herself on that gurney years back—alone and in pain, bleeding and suffering badly.

Her knees grew weak at the memory, and she leaned against the wall for support. God, it had been so hard. That terrible fear, the awful pain. The misery of losing her child. The worry that she'd somehow caused it.

The absolute devastation of knowing Cade would rather leap from airplanes than stay with her.

But that wasn't true. Cade hadn't abandoned her.

She blinked as reality came seeping back, and with it, the truth. Cade wasn't like her father. He would have rushed to her side.

She was the one at fault. She hadn't trusted him or his love, hadn't given him a chance to help her. Then she'd left him without explanation and blamed him for her mistakes.

How could she have been so foolish?

Her blood still slamming in her ears, she struggled to regain her composure. Just then two women rushed past.

"We're right behind you, Tommy," one woman called.

Jordan watched them scurry into the curtained space behind the gurney, and then another truth rocked through her. Unlike her, that man wasn't alone. He had friends to visit him, a support group, people eager to help—whereas Jordan had cut herself off from society back then. Even when they'd moved to Missoula, she hadn't tried to fit in.

A bitter taste wedged in her throat. She didn't like that glimpse of herself, but she had to admit it was true. She hadn't made friends. She'd used her childhood as an excuse to withdraw from people, then blamed Cade for leaving her alone.

She closed her eyes. How could she have been so immature? Hadn't she done anything right?

Still reeling from this view of her past, she opened her eyes and hobbled off. The bay doors opened with a quiet whoosh as she limped from the emergency room into the lobby, and then out the hospital's main entrance. The automatic doors slid open to the dark night and a blast of cool air.

She worked her way to the curb, stopped and stared

at the near-empty lot. So here she was again, alone. She didn't have family or friends in Missoula, didn't know anyone who could help her, aside from Cade. And she had nowhere left to go.

And that was her own damned fault.

She stumbled to a bench beneath a light pole and sat. Moths swarmed above her in the halogen haze. A few cars passed on the nearby road, people going home to waiting families. But no one was expecting her. She didn't have that family she'd always longed for or the husband she'd always desired.

Because she'd pushed him away.

Her throat cramped with another spasm, and she blinked furiously to stem the hot tears. She'd messed up everything, all right. She'd wounded the man she'd loved and destroyed his trust.

But she couldn't alter the past. And she couldn't just sit here and weep. She wasn't that weak girl anymore, and those helpless days were long gone. She sniffed back her tears and thought hard.

She could check herself into a motel, the same one she'd stayed in when she'd first arrived. She could take a taxi there and spend the night. Then, in the morning, she could resolve the rental car problem and take the first available flight back East.

But why bother? What did she have waiting in Virginia, aside from her job? She loved her work and had built herself a solid career, but nursing homes existed all over. She could find another job here if she decided to stay. Plus, she no longer had a boyfriend there; she couldn't date Phil when she still loved Cade.

An ache pulsed down her throat at the thought of Cade, followed by a spurt of dread. She needed to break up with Phil. He was a kind, decent man, and she couldn't lead him on any longer. No matter how distasteful the task, she had to tell him the truth.

She pulled her cell phone from her bag and turned it on, glad that the battery still worked. Then she paused. She couldn't do it this way, not by phone. It wasn't fair to Phil. She'd be taking the coward's way out, running from her problems again.

And she wasn't doing that anymore. She wasn't that scared, immature girl; she was an adult, and she would face her problems head-on.

Which meant she had to tell Phil in person.

And then she had to decide what to do with her life.

A sharp, heavy longing pressed on her heart. God, she missed Cade. Only a few hours apart and already she couldn't stand it. She missed his eyes, that rumbling voice, that sexy, confident grin. How could she bear to spend her life without him?

Was there any chance he would forgive her? She'd hurt him so badly and ruined the trust between them. Could she convince him that she'd changed?

She had to try.

Because she really wasn't that young girl anymore. She'd changed over the years. She'd proven that up on the mountain. She'd forded a river and battled a cougar. She'd hiked miles on a wounded ankle and escaped a raging fire.

And no way was she now slinking out of Montana without fighting for the man she loved.

Just then, her cell phone beeped, and she held it up to the light. A text message had arrived from Phil.

Surprised, she punched the buttons to retrieve the message. Then she blinked. Phil was here in Missoula, waiting at her motel. He'd heard about the fire and had come to find her.

Her astonishment turned to dismay, and then settled into resolve. She hadn't expected him here, but his arrival couldn't be better. First, she would meet with him, explain that she didn't love him and that he deserved a more suitable wife.

Then she'd track down the man she did love and plead for a second chance.

An hour later, she stood in front of Phil's motel room and balanced her crutches on the faded red carpet. Muted voices from the television seeped through the door, so she knew that he was awake. She knocked, sending a loud rap echoing down the deserted hallway, then winced, hoping she wouldn't disturb the neighbors. It was after midnight, too late for a social call, but past time to own up to her mistakes.

Seconds later, the security chain rattled, and then the door swung open and Phil stepped into view. His brown eyes blinked behind his wire-rimmed glasses. "Jordan?"

"Hi, Phil." Warmth slid through her chest, along with a strong spurt of fondness, the delight at seeing a friend. There was no nervous anticipation, none of the thrilling jolts she felt whenever she saw Cade.

"Holy cow." His jaw slack, he opened the door wider. His eyes grew dazed as he scanned from her torn jeans and dirty face to the bandages on her hands. "What happened to you?"

"I got caught in the fire."

"Oh, man. I was afraid of that. Are you okay?"

"I'm fine."

He stepped forward and opened his arms, then enveloped her in a hug. "Stop," she protested. "I'll get you dirty."

But he squeezed her anyway, surrounding her with his strength. And she realized that it was this friendship, this dependability that she had confused with love. He was a safe and solid man.

Just not the right one for her.

"I came as soon as I heard about the fire," he said, pulling away. "No one knew where you were, and I was going nuts trying to get news."

He surveyed her, worry creasing his brow. His khaki slacks were wrinkled, his polo shirt askew. His normally neat hair was mussed, as if he'd tugged each strand from its place.

"I can't believe this," he continued. "You look…"

"Filthy, I know." And like the fire survivor she was, bruised and battered, smeared with ashes and grime. Her matted hair tumbled wildly over her shoulders, and she reeked of smoke and sweat.

"And you've got crutches," he noted, still looking stunned.

"It's just a sprained ankle. Nothing serious." She gazed into his familiar face and felt his warmth and concern.

A weight loosened around her heart, and any doubts she might have harbored vanished. And suddenly she felt free, liberated, as if a burden had disappeared from her life.

How could she have thought she loved this man? He was so obviously wrong for her—perfectly nice, and the best of friends, but nothing more than that.

As much as she cared for him, she didn't feel that spark, that depth of feeling she had for Cade. And after her soul-searching up on that mountain, she refused to settle for anything less. She didn't want a stale, predictable life any longer. She didn't want a diet of bland white bread and vanilla ice cream, no matter how comfortable the taste.

She wanted excitement, fireworks, passion.

She wanted Cade, smokejumping career and all.

"Phil, I—" She sighed, knowing that this would be hard. "Listen, we need to talk. But it's a long story, and I need to shower first. I've got a room down the hall." She nodded in that direction. "Can we meet in an hour to talk?"

"Sure." He stared at her charred jeans, still looking dazed. Then he snapped his gaze back up. "Are you hungry? We can see if anything's open and grab something to eat."

"I'd like that." A surge of affection warmed her heart. No matter what, Phil had flown out here because he cared. And that's what she called a good friend. "And Phil?"

He raised his brows, still looking shell-shocked.

"I appreciate that you came to find me."

"Sure." He blinked again, and she hobbled away.

Chapter 17

"McKenzie! What are you doing here?"

Trying like hell to forget about Jordan. Cade leaned against a long table in the parachute loft as his smoke-jumping bro, Trey Campbell, strolled toward him. Not that he'd managed to stop thinking about her yet. That woman had worked herself under his skin, driving herself in so deeply that it hurt him even to breathe.

But no way was he admitting that to Trey. His bro had witnessed the hell he'd suffered the first time Jordan had dumped him, and had spent months trying to help him stay sane. No way could he confess that he'd let her destroy him again.

The dog trailed Trey into the loft. When he spotted Cade, he wagged his tail and rushed to greet him.

Careful not to bump his arm, which was secured in a harness-style sling, Cade squatted to ruffle his fur.

The dog looked different this morning, more civilized. His fur had been washed and brushed, his nails trimmed, and he sported a blue bandanna. And he didn't stink anymore. "Hey, buddy," Cade said. "Looks like somebody groomed you."

"No kidding." Trey propped his hip against the opposite table. "What did that mutt do, anyhow? Roll in a rotting carcass?"

"Beats me." Cade gave the dog a final pat and straightened while Trey nodded to the other jumpers in the loft. The master rigger sat at one of the sewing machines below the row of elk heads lining the wall, a blue-and-white parachute spread over his legs. There was a lull in the whir of his sewing machine as he greeted Trey back.

"Yo, Trey," another rigger called above the blare of country music. "You at the top of the list yet?"

"Getting close," Trey said. "I should make the second load."

"Sounds good." The rigger finished packing a chute and pushed it down the long table toward Cade.

Cade reached around a spare iron and glue gun, and picked it up. He checked the size, then strode over and stuffed it into the green cubicle along the wall with the other mediums. With fires popping up all over, they needed to keep the shelves stocked.

Which was why he'd rationalized coming back to work today. At this time of year, they needed all the help they could get. Unfortunately, no matter how busy he stayed, he couldn't keep his mind off Jordan.

"I thought you were supposed to take it easy for a while," Trey said.

"Hell, this *is* easy." He slouched back against the table. "Not much else I can do with a broken collarbone and two cracked ribs."

"Except stay in bed?"

"Right." And no way was he doing that. Every time he closed his eyes, those damned memories flashed through his brain, of Jordan's smile, her silky skin, that amazing sex in the cave.

So, after a sleepless night spent battling the need to see her, he'd given up and headed to the base. He knew he'd go crazy if he didn't find something to distract him.

"So what happened up on that mountain?" Trey persisted, crossing his arms.

"Nothing much." Cade kept his expression neutral. "We found the dog, the fire blew up, they flew us out."

"Uh-huh." Trey's shrewd eyes narrowed. "And that's why you bolted out of that hospital before I could get back to pick you up?"

"I didn't bolt." Not exactly. He scowled. "Hell, you saw what I looked like. I probably smelled worse than the dog. I just wanted to shower and eat."

And get away from Jordan before he did something foolish, like begging her to love him again.

"Uh-huh," Trey repeated, his smirk indicating he wasn't fooled.

Damning Trey for being too perceptive, Cade strode from the loft into the inspection tower, the dog cheerfully tagging his heels. He muttered a greeting to the loft foreman, who was staring up at a red-and-white reserve chute hanging from the ceiling, then pushed his way past the looping shroud lines and anti-inversion netting dangling off the blue-and-white mains.

He glanced down to make sure the dog stayed with him and mentally sighed. Okay, so maybe Trey was right. He *had* fled the hospital. He hadn't trusted himself around Jordan. He knew if he gave her the chance, she'd worm her way back into his soul and capture his heart.

Hell, who was he fooling? She already had.

But at least he'd had the sense to control the damage this time. He'd gotten away before he lost all common sense and begged her to stay.

So why wasn't he relieved? He should be glad he'd escaped that danger.

He braced himself, expecting to feel the rush of anger, the sense of betrayal she always evoked, but he couldn't conjure it up this time. His rage had dwindled during the night, mellowing into something new.

Guilt.

Guilt that she'd suffered that miscarriage and he hadn't been there to help. Remorse that he hadn't eased the pain or kept her safe.

Not that he'd had much chance. She hadn't even told him she was pregnant. Still, he'd been her husband. He should have been at her side.

His gut knotted, his emotions slugging hard through his chest, he strode into the ready room and glanced around. His gaze landed on the jump list posted by the dispatch desk, and he automatically started to scan it.

He'd traveled halfway through the second column before he caught himself. The green magnetic tag bearing his name had been scuttled off to the side, where it would stay for the rest of the season. He had to get used to that fact.

And find some other way to keep his mind off Jordan.

Several jumpers milled around the ready room, repacking their personal gear bags and checking their equipment. Keeping a close watch on the dog in case the siren blew, Cade wandered to his locker and looked in. His jumpsuit jacket hung on one hook, his helmet and pants on another. He made a mental note to thank Trey for returning his gear.

Even if he wouldn't need it until next spring.

"Hey, Cade." The rookie he'd saved knelt nearby, stuffing a can of baked beans into his PG bag. The kid stood, stuck his bag beneath the shelf in the narrow locker, then strolled over to Cade. "Sorry about your shoulder. I heard it's messed up pretty bad."

"The bone's just cracked. Nothing major." It was a hell of a way to end the season, but at least the injury would heal.

Grimacing, the kid rubbed the back of his neck. "Yeah, well, thanks again, man. For pushing me out of the way, I mean."

"No problem."

"I still can't believe I froze like that."

Cade shrugged his uninjured shoulder. "Don't sweat it. We all make mistakes." Sometimes the same one twice.

"I guess so." The rookie motioned toward the far wall. "But maybe next time, I'll remember the sign."

Cade glanced back at the bright yellow sign posted near the jump list. It warned in big black letters that Stupid Hurts.

His lips twisted. Stupid hurt, all right. Even knowing better, he'd let Jordan trample his heart.

"Well, anyway," the rookie continued. "I owe you, man. Big-time."

"Just buy me a drink next time you're back this way."

"It's a deal." The rookie grinned, his smile wide in his cleanly shaved face, and Cade noticed how young he looked, hardly over twenty.

Which made him suddenly feel old.

Just then the siren blared, ending their conversation, and they both turned toward the operations desk. Cade felt the familiar surge of adrenaline, followed by a swift jab of disappointment. His name wasn't on that list.

The siren faded, and the operations foreman grabbed the mike. "We have a twelve-person jump request to the Bob Marshall Wilderness," he announced. He turned to the jump list on the wall beside him. "Jumpers will be Susan Jennings, Jim Scibert, Rick Crossley . . ."

"Got to go!" The rookie darted to his locker, yanked out his Kevlar jump pants and rammed his legs inside.

The foreman finished reading the list, and people streamed into the ready room, instantly engulfing it in controlled commotion. Those not leaving began helping the jumpers suit up. Others snapped on parachutes and handed off gear. Everyone worked as a team to get the jumpers on the plane and off to the fire with lightning speed.

Feeling useless and in the way with his bum arm, Cade called the dog and moved outside to the ramp. He strolled past the shelves stocked with para cargo—climbing spurs and trauma kits, freeze-dried food and cubes of water—then leaned against a crate in the shade to watch the action. One by one, the jumpers staggered out of the ready room to the waiting Twin Otter, barely staying upright under the weight of their equipment.

A minute later, Trey wandered out and joined him in the shade. The Otter's engine whined as the pilot prepared for takeoff. The spotter stood outside the door performing last-minute safety checks before the jumpers climbed on board. Cade felt the excitement in the air, the anticipation, and wished to hell he could get on that plane.

"Where are you on the list?" he asked Trey.

"About ten down now. I should make the next load."

"Lucky man." Cade sucked in a breath of jet fumes and blew it out.

"Yeah. This is turning into a great season for overtime pay." He shot Cade an apologetic smile. "Hell of a time to get injured."

"Yeah." It was, but the risks were part of the job.

Trey tilted his head. "You planning on keeping the dog?"

Cade turned slightly to glance at the mutt, who was nosing around the trash can in the corner. And he remembered how Jordan had protected that dog, carrying him through the river and across the fire, even defying a mountain lion to save him.

A weight pressed down on his heart. "I don't have much choice. He saved my life. The least I can do is feed him."

"Have fun. That mutt ate three burgers and a large order of fries last night."

Cade blinked. "You took him out for hamburgers?"

"Hey, it was a special occasion."

Cade raised his brows.

"His first bath?"

"Right." Cade shook his head and grinned, doubting Jordan would approve of that diet. But Jordan would never know what the dog ate. A swift cramp rent his heart, blocking his breath. Damn, he needed to get her out of his head.

Just then the rookie swaggered by on his way to the plane. "Thanks again, McKenzie," he called. Then he laughed and said something to a female bro, his face beaming with excitement.

Cade shook his head again. "Man, those rookies look young."

"We were the same age when we started."

"Twenty-three." And he could still remember how desperately he'd wanted to become a smokejumper, to belong to the firefighting elite. He'd worked like hell to get through rookie training, and he'd been so damned proud when he'd made it.

"You remember that trip to Cancún?" Trey asked.

"How could I forget it?" They'd headed down to Mexico right after that first season had ended, intending to have some fun. Two kick-ass smokejumpers out to raise hell on the beach.

And then he'd met Jordan.

She'd been even younger than he was, just out of high school. And his heart had fallen fast.

The last jumper climbed into the Otter, and the spotter leaped aboard. Seconds later, the plane turned and rolled down the runway. The engines screamed as it picked up speed and lifted off.

Cade watched it head toward the distant mountains and disappear into the hot blue haze. He loved that moment when the plane took off, when he was soaring into the sky toward adventure, never knowing what would await him or what incredible sights he might see.

Living the smokejumper dream.

"Easy to make mistakes at that age," Trey said.

"I guess." Cade tugged his attention back to earth and touched his sling. The rookie had made a mistake, all right, taking him out for the season. But everyone screwed up sometimes.

Even him. And he'd screwed up big-time with Jordan.

"I always liked her, you know," Trey added. "I figured she must have had a reason to leave."

Cade didn't pretend not to understand. It was obvious he was talking about Jordan. He squinted out at the hazy sky. "She had a miscarriage."

"Yeah? You never told me she was pregnant."

"I didn't know."

Neither spoke for several moments. A bro laughed from inside the building. In the distance, a car door slammed. The dog wandered over and sniffed the bicycle parked near the crates.

"That must have been rough on her," Trey finally said.

"Yeah." Cade's chest squeezed as he pictured the scene. Jordan lying in the hospital, scared and alone, her beautiful eyes black with terror, her face as pale as the sheets.

He fisted his hand, knowing how much she had suffered, imagining her fierce pain and grief.

And she'd been so damn young. Hell. Could he really blame her for bolting?

Guilt slid through his gut. He'd hardly been perfect. He'd been full of himself back then, cocky, just like the rookie he'd saved. Too caught up in the thrill of smokejumping to notice her needs.

He should have paid more attention. He never should have brushed her complaints or fears aside.

And he should have discussed his decision to join that booster crew with her. They'd been married, for God's sake, but he'd still acted as if he were single.

Remorse soured his gut. So he wasn't blameless. She'd been right about that.

And she'd been right about something else. They hadn't talked enough. They'd both made assumptions that had ruined their marriage. He'd figured she could cope on her own. She'd thought he only cared about his job.

"I was in Alaska when it happened," he said.

"Living the dream."

"Right." The twist of his lips was sardonic. But was it really a dream if it had cost him Jordan? Was any job, even this one, worth losing the woman he loved?

He squinted into the sunny haze. Back when he'd first started, he'd thought so. Smokejumping was everything to him. It was what he was born to do and the first place he'd ever belonged. And nothing could have stopped him from jumping.

But in the end, was it worth the price? Did fighting fire matter more to him than Jordan?

The truth slammed into him then, knocking the air from his lungs. He'd been wrong. God, he'd been wrong. He needed Jordan far more than any job. He always had.

Sure he liked smokejumping, and it would pain him to give it up, but he could do something else. He could become a dispatcher or base foreman, train rookies or rig parachutes. This wasn't the only job where he could excel.

But he couldn't survive without Jordan. She completed him and made him whole. She loved him, cared for him in a way no one else ever could.

And she mattered far more to him than smokejumping ever had.

His gut cramped, and a fierce desperation seized him. He had to find her and stop her from leaving. He had to apologize and plead for another chance.

But where could he find her? He didn't know which motel she'd stayed in, or even if she'd stayed in town overnight. For all he knew, she could have taken a red-eye flight from Missoula and be back in Virginia by now.

Panicked, he turned around.

"You need a ride somewhere, McKenzie?" Trey rubbed his jaw, not quite hiding his smirk.

"Yeah." Cade blew out his breath. No one hid anything from the bros. "But you're too high on the jump list. I'll bum a ride from someone else." Although where he'd look for Jordan, he didn't know.

He whistled, and the dog trotted over. "Did you happen to buy a leash?"

"Right here." Trey pulled a coiled leash from his pocket, snapped it onto the collar beneath the dog's bandanna and handed the end to Cade. "You're sure you want to take the dog with you?"

"Oh, yeah." This mutt had saved his life up on that mountain. Maybe now he could help rescue his heart.

Chapter 18

The taxi pulled to the curb in front of the smoke-jumper base and stopped. Her heart flipping erratically, Jordan scanned the familiar one-story complex fronting the shimmering tarmac. Mountains framed the horizon beyond the airfield, their high peaks melting into the haze.

A tour group gathered in front of the gift-shop door, chatting and angling their cameras at the buildings. A sprinkler launched water onto the parched grass, its ticking swoosh rhythmic in the morning sun. The scent of freshly mown grass rose in the hot Montana breeze, triggering memories of the times she'd come here with Cade.

But she didn't feel that bitterness anymore, that old sense of loss that being at the base once evoked. She felt at peace now, settled and filled with a sense of rightness.

She'd finally accomplished what she'd set out to do. She'd banished those old ghosts.

Just not the ones she had expected.

"Is this the right place?" the taxi driver asked.

"Yes." It was definitely the right place. It had been a long journey back here, years filled with resentment and misunderstanding, painful growth and change. But she was finally back where she was supposed to be.

"You want me to wait?"

"No, I'm fine." She pulled her wallet from her purse and handed him a bill. "You can keep the change," she added.

"Thanks." While the driver leaped out and came around the car, she collected her purse and bag, opened her door and slid from the seat. He took her crutches from the rear seat and handed them over.

She propped them under her arms. At least Phil had taken the breakup better than she'd expected. He'd been wounded at first, due to the blow to his pride. But then he'd admitted that he'd sensed this might happen. And in a way, he was relieved.

Because truthfully, she'd changed since they'd first started dating. She wasn't the dependent, security-seeking woman he'd first asked out. And now that they both understood that, they made far better friends than potential lovers.

Just then the side door of the parachute loft opened and a smokejumper strode out with a dog. *Her* dog. Her gaze flew to the man's handsome face. Her heart tripped, then started quaking.

Cade. Oh, God.

Her nerves leaped like a crowning wildfire. Her

pulse rocketed like that blowup blasting uphill. Her breath backed up in her lungs, and she couldn't suck in the dense air.

His eyes met hers from across the yard and he stopped. Time faltered, then stretched to a standstill. The world around them faded and blurred.

Frozen in place, she just stared at him, her gaze devouring every detail. The spiked blond hair fringing the solid cords of his neck. The iron strength of his biceps beneath the black T-shirt. The olive-drab pants hanging low on his hips and the sling cradling his arm. He looked rugged and brave, and so god-awful sexy that she ached to rush over and hug him.

"Is that everything?" the driver asked.

"Yes," she whispered, still trapped by those dazzling eyes. Cade was everything, all right. He was the man she'd been destined to love.

She couldn't read his expression from where she stood, couldn't tell if he would give her a chance to explain. But at least he hadn't turned away yet. Hope surged hard in her chest.

The dog jumped and strained against the leash, then let out a welcoming yip. Without taking his gaze from hers, Cade started striding forward.

Her stomach clenched in a rush of nerves. Even if Cade agreed to hear her out, he might never forgive her. She now knew how badly she'd acted. But she was going to try.

The driver cranked the engine and pulled away from the curb, and she glanced at the departing cab. Another ending. She'd had enough of those in her life.

Her throat balled, and she turned back to Cade. Now

it was time for a new start, another beginning. And this one mattered most of all.

Her heart thrumming, she adjusted her crutches and hobbled toward him. They met on the grass halfway to the loft. She stopped just inches away, the air so thick now she couldn't breathe.

He flicked his gaze over her, and her heart made a long, slow roll in her chest. Their eyes latched again, and she felt the familiar hum of awareness, the intensity and heat.

And she couldn't tear her gaze away.

"Hey," he murmured. His low, husky voice raised the hair on her arms, like a shiver on the warm wind. "You're looking good."

Her lips curved. "Cleaner, anyway." He looked more than good, and she longed to wrap herself around him, to caress those gorgeous muscles and taste the feverish heat of his skin. To stoke that hunger that drove them both wild.

But she had something to say first. Jerking her mind back to her mission, she swallowed hard. "Cade, I…I wanted to tell you, I—"

Dusty bumped her leg, then leaped up and braced his paws on her chest. She staggered on her crutches to keep her balance.

"Whoa, there." Cade lunged forward and grabbed her arm, and his hot touch seared though her skin.

She shivered hard. "I'm okay," she breathed. The dog dropped his paws, and Cade slowly released her arm.

She moved aside her crutches so she could bend down and pet the dog. She scratched beneath his ears, and smiled when he let out a whine. "He looks nice all clean and brushed. And I like his bandanna." It gave him a rakish look.

"The bros got it. They like him."

"That's good." She sucked in her breath and slowly straightened. "Listen, Cade, I came to tell you I..."

His gaze slammed into hers again, so intense that she couldn't think. Waves of desire crashed through her, wedging the air in her throat. Dear God, how she loved this man. "I, uh..."

"What?" His eyes narrowed, the heat only slightly banked.

Her pulse tripped, then sprinted through her veins. "I wanted to tell you, I..."

She stopped and dragged in a breath. She had to get a grip. She was mucking this all up, not even making sense.

Then the tour group wandered past, staring and smiling at Cade, and stopped on the nearby sidewalk. The tour guide joined them, and the visitors clustered around, eager to hear about the smokejumper life.

"Why don't we sit in the shade?" Cade suggested.

"Good idea." She didn't want an audience when she bared her soul.

"I'll take your bag," he said.

"I can handle it."

"I know."

His gaze met hers, and his mouth slid into a grin. That sexy, soul-pounding grin. The thumping of her pulse grew faster.

"Thanks." She handed him the bag.

They walked silently across the road toward a small, shaded park, Dusty trotting between them. A picnic table sat under a cottonwood tree, near the antique lookout display. The parking lot bordered one side, the frontage road another, partially sheltering them from prying eyes.

She lowered herself to the bench, facing the road. Cade sat down beside her, and she propped her crutches against the table. Dusty dropped to the grass at their feet.

She reached down again and scratched the dog's ears, wondering how to begin. He swished his tail along the grass and licked her hand, and a spurt of warmth mellowed her heart. At least he had a better life.

But would she?

Her heart trembling, she sat back. This was it, the moment of truth. She dragged in her breath and met his gaze. "I came here because I was hoping that we, that maybe… I mean, I know I don't deserve it, but I love you and…" Her breath hitched. "Oh, God, Cade—"

"Jordan." His deep voice stopped her.

He reached over and picked up her hand, and the air in her lungs stalled. He cradled her hand in his bigger one, his rough calluses tingling the skin around her bandage. Scars branched from his fingers to his forearm, testimony to years spent working in the forests. His tendons flexed with power and strength.

How could she have ever doubted that she could depend on this man?

"I was just heading out to look for you," he said.

"You were?" Her heart abruptly lost its rhythm.

"Yeah." He stared at their joined hands. He stroked her wrist with his thumb, sending shivers along her nerves, then threaded his lean fingers with hers. "I wanted to ask you for another chance."

Her heart stuttered. Her pulse made a long, hard beat through her skull, then hammered in her ears.

He still wanted her. Tears swelled in her eyes, and she blinked to clear them away.

"I'm so sorry," she whispered, her throat so cramped she could barely speak. "I was such a fool. And I messed everything up."

A sad, tight smile twisted his lips, and he tightened his grip on her hand. "I'm the one who should apologize. You were right, what you said before. I should have talked to you more. And I did care too much about my job."

He released her hand and shifted to face her. She hardly breathed as he traced the bruise along her cheek, his rough, warm fingers sparking on her skin.

"I plan to quit if you'll take me back," he said.

Her lungs ceased. The world around them slanted. "You'd do that for me?" she gasped. "You'd really quit your job?"

"Yeah." He lowered his hand and switched his gaze to the road. A motorcycle passed, its reverberations fading as it headed toward the mountains.

When the noise died out, he sighed. "It took me a while, but I finally figured it out. When I first started smokejumping, I wanted to prove that I could do it, that I belonged here. That I could succeed in this world. But I don't need that anymore."

His gaze met hers. "Don't get me wrong. I like the work, the bros, but the job's not everything to me anymore. I can be happy doing something else."

He tugged her hand into his. "I love you, Jordan. I missed you so damned much. And I don't want to lose you again. You matter more than any job."

A sob rose in her throat. Her heart swelled with an ache so huge that she could barely speak. "That's the nicest thing anyone has ever done for me," she whispered. It was what she'd always wanted, what she'd dreamed. "But I don't want you to quit."

"Jordan—"

"No, listen." She shook his hand loose, and swiped at her brimming eyes with her sleeve. "I've thought about this a lot, about my childhood. How I spent years watching those ships disappear, looking out to sea.

"And I thought about our marriage. About how lonely I was and especially what I did wrong, like not making friends.

"And I asked myself whether, honestly, I could do it again, whether I could survive that lifestyle this time. And I realized I could."

"Jordan—"

"No, wait." She needed him to understand. "Remember how I told you about my job, about the elderly people I work with? How they aren't afraid of dying? They don't focus on the negative part, on the short time they have left. They celebrate what they do have, their moments together, and they live each day as a gift.

"And maybe I won't like having you gone in the summer, but it won't bother me like it did before." She would have her work to fill her time, dogs to rescue, and maybe someday, another child.

She shrugged. "I don't know why it seemed so hard

before. Maybe we just didn't talk enough. Maybe I was too young, and I didn't really know who I was.

"But I've changed. I'm not the same person I used to be. I'm stronger."

"Yeah." He stroked the line of her jaw, scorching her with his heat. "But I still don't mind changing jobs."

"I know. And maybe someday you should. But I fell in love with a smokejumper." She understood that now. It was part of his identity, who he was, a man who risked his life to fight fires. She held his gaze. "And I don't want you to change who you are."

His gaze sizzled into hers, sparking that hot, slow burn in her blood. "You're sure?"

"Absolutely."

"So you'll marry me again?"

"Oh, yes." He had her heart and soul forever. "And this time, I'm here to stay."

* * * * *